AGELESS
OBSESSION

AGELESS OBSESSION

A Melody Fox Mystery

Beverly Ungar

SUNSTONE
PRESS

SANTA FE

*The events, people, and incidents in this story are the sole product
of the author's imagination. The story is fictional and any resemblance
to individuals living or dead is purely coincidental.*

Cover photograph by Carl Condit
Author's photograph by Kim Kurian

Sunstone books may be purchased for educational, business, or sales promotional use.
For information please write: Special Markets Department, Sunstone Press,
P.O. Box 2321, Santa Fe, New Mexico 87504-2321.

Library of Congress Cataloging-in-Publication Data:

Ungar, Beverly, 1946–
   Ageless obsession / by Beverly Ungar.
      p. cm.
   ISBN: 0-86534-417-5 (hardcover)   ISBN: 0-86534-378-0 (pbk.)
   1. Women psychologists—Fiction. 2. Biotechnology—Fiction. I. Title.

PS 3621.N48 A73 2003
813'.6—dc22

                        2003017931

Published in
Santa Fe

WWW.SUNSTONEPRESS.COM
POST OFFICE BOX 2321 / SANTA FE, NM 87504-2321 / USA
(505) 988-4418 / ORDERS ONLY (800) 243-5644 / FAX (505) 988-1025

To my wonderful mother,
Beatrice Geifman

With sincere thanks to Deborah and Elizabeth Ungar,
Nancy Hartlaub, Sue Pelley, Babs Treiber,
Vicki Arnold, Venise Berry, Stephen Greenleaf,
and Jim Northup for your help and inspiration.

1

"Amen," the large crowd gathered at the cemetery repeated in bereaved unison. Softly hushed sobs and sniffles punctuated the reflective solitude of mourners — some seated, some standing under the lapiz blue canopy.

Grant Fisher's funeral was the most stirring and inspiring funeral Melody Fox had ever observed. In truth, it was the only funeral Melody had ever attended in her halcyon thirty-five years. Her life up until now had been blessed.

Suddenly, without a warning the flawless azure, Arizona sky dimmed, darkened, then eclipsed into a churning, stormy gray. It threatened and roiled turbulently over and into itself until the sky turned from dismal gray to impenetrable blue black. Lightning burned a luminant vein of brilliant white through the night-like sky. Thunder rumbled and crashed, instantly reverberating through the crowd that was gathered to say goodbye to Grant Fisher, husband, father, and successful businessman.

Just then another booming thunderous crackle rolled into the mountains less than a mile from the mourners then bounced back, embracing them all in its eerie echo. The heavy clouds let loose and pelted cold, piercing rain, blown sideways by a wild wind that whipped out of nowhere. But in the next minute or so the storm was over and gone as inexplicably as it had begun. It seemed as though time had become severed from any sense of reality. The air throbbed in thick silence.

No one so much as breathed or blinked, mesmerized in an aura of timelessness and incredulity. Mourners gazed at each other mystified, trying to comprehend the awesome display of nature's profound vagaries.

Suddenly, hauntingly quiet, the sun reappeared, at first timidly as the clouds dispersed, then brazenly, radiating brightly. The bold light beamed intently on Grant Fisher's widow and two small boys, his family, friends, and business associates. One final, menacingly long low thunder rumbled across the now flawlessly clear blue sky. Melody Fox could swear Grant Fisher was bellowing one final outcry—cautioning that something wasn't as it seemed.

Feeling uneasy, Melody suddenly noticed the stabbing glare of someone whose face she recognized but couldn't place in her cache of memories. The woman looking at her appeared to be about the same age as Melody, perhaps a bit younger. Contentiousness seemed to ooze through the woman's efforts at hiding the emotion. There were little lines around the woman's eyes that Melody guessed were from squinting perpetual disapproval of everyone around her.

Although petulance prevailed on her face, it did little to subdue her striking beauty. Her emerald eyes radiated health, vigor, and the intensity of a cougar. Her enviable skin was clear and touched with vibrancy. Her pout emphasized full, soft, sensuous lips. Various flavors of blonde—flax, corn, wheat, and honey—flowed like spring sunshine to her shoulders with only a hint of darker roots. Whoever she was, Melody didn't ever want to have to tangle with her. She appeared to be a spoiled, formidable bitch who took having whatever she wanted in stride.

Melody shot the woman a quick smile—a mocking display of friendship in an attempt to crack the woman's composure. It was the most contrary response Melody could think of to unbalance the pompous stranger scrutinizing her.

"Who's that blonde woman glaring at me?" Melody asked her husband Stuart, being careful so the woman couldn't read her lips.

"Laurel," Stuart answered without another word.

Well, that certainly explained everything! Of course Laurel would be at Grant's funeral. Stuart had been married to Laurel for about a heartbeat shortly after he and Grant started their advertising agency. Although their marriage lasted less than a year, of course her husband's ex-wife would be here now, mourning the man who had been Stuart's partner. Still, Melody felt Laurel's silent acidic impertinence uncalled for, especially at this somber ceremony.

There were countless other mourners Melody didn't know. Friends and neighbors of Marisa and Grant, plus business associates and clients of Fisher and Fox Advertising Agency. Another strikingly beautiful woman was attached to a group of professionals who had come to the funeral as a pack. She was dressed in a superbly cut, obviously expensive eggplant purple silk suit and snatched furtive looks at her watch at least every other second. This woman was petite and dark. Dark hair, dark eyes. A young Elizabeth Taylor kind of beauty with a no-nonsense composure. The men she was with were all business and it was easy to tell by their stiff body language that they would have preferred to be elsewhere.

"Who's the woman in the purple suit?"

Stuart shrugged his shoulders.

Finally, the casket was lowered into the grave accompanied by the thuds of dirt dropped in heart-throbbingly repetitious shovelfuls by solemn mourning relatives. The smell of freshly turned dirt smattered by the recent rain was an odor that, until this moment, Melody had always associated with spring and resurgence. Now, as the wind whisked the scent of wet earth up to her nostrils, Melody was jerked back to the present solemnity of this funeral gathering.

Melody and Stuart Fox exchanged no more words as they stood on the outskirts of the Fisher family group remaining by the grave, sharing the deep and painful void that would never be filled. Marisa Fisher, her two young sons, her parents, sister, and brother-in-law, as well as Grant's parents, brothers, and sisters-in-law finally turned their backs to the grave, their faces toward the forever changed world that would now be theirs to live in.

Melody and Stuart joined the family and together gave Marisa a wordless, heartfelt hug.

There was still the meal of condolence to share with the mourners on this sad day.

"Please come over to the house later. I'd like you two there. Okay?" Marisa requested while her sad eyes implored.

"Sure. 'Course," Stuart answered. "We'll be there."

Afterwards, still spellbound from the strange brief storm, everyone headed to their cars. Melody held her husband's hand as they walked silently through the cemetery. She tried hard not to picture what it would be like if it had been Stuart instead of Grant who had died of a heart attack Sunday. She and Stuart were still head over heals in love after being married for just over five years.

"He was only forty-two, Melody. The same age as me," Stuart said quietly, expressing Melody's exact thoughts. "You expect a lot of days and years left when you're forty-two. You don't expect to die suddenly of a heart attack without any warning." Stuart was tortured by the events of the last four days. "Sunday Grant was jogging and today he was buried. How could this happen?"

There aren't any answers beyond silence to questions about mortality.

Until four days ago, Grant Fisher and Stuart Fox had been partners in a business they started together ten years ago after a drunken night of angry toasts to their former boss. They had been fired after an outrageously irreverent but on-the-money presentation to an important client. The client hated it, the conservative agency owner who had originally approved the presentation let the two 'young guys' take the fall. After their termination, they'd headed straight to Buster's where rudimentary images of their own business began to unfold.

"Fuck 'em," had been Grant and Stuart's most often repeated toast that prodigious night sitting in the bar. The two cohorts who worked together, who really didn't know each other beyond the confines of their cubicles, began planning a partnership influenced by the bravery of countless celebratory scotches. Maybe not seriously. In the haze of liquor induced brilliance or lunacy, depending on how you looked at it, starting their own agency seemed like a perfectly logical if not practical idea. It became a now or never endeavor with the urgency of a meticulously timed rocket launch. It was a possibility – the beginning of a dream they had each secretly held: one day owning their own advertising agency. Grant and Stuart were both young, smart, capable, creative.

"Both brilliant, " toasted Grant.

"Both clever," pledged Stuart.

"Shrewd."

"Witty."

"Good looking."

"Damn good looking."

"Unemployed."

After vociferously celebrating their self-proclaimed virtues, once the truth was brazenly uttered that evening, their laughter came to an abrupt end and was replaced by a silence filled with pensive musing. Not another word was said and each went home to face tomorrow, unemployed.

The Fisher and Fox Agency started out small with only three clients but it was huge if measured by hopefulness. It quickly grew to a staff of twelve with local, regional, and national awards lining the walls of the agency's entryway. Grant and Stuart actually were, as they had declared that long ago night, clever, shrewd, creative, witty, and smart. They were young, professional, successful stars in their field.

Thursday, the evening of the long day of the funeral, Melody and Stuart tried their best to console Marisa by clinging to happy memories of earlier times. They laughed, reminiscing over silly episodes instigated by Grant, and cried about things that would never be. It was blatantly obvious to both Stuart and Melody that Marisa needed to talk some more about the day it all happened, and they were compassionate listeners.

"I remember when Grant came in and collapsed in that chair Sunday thinking that he'd run too far too fast in too much heat. Grant was young and healthy." Tears were welling in Marisa's eyes although behind the tears loomed a brilliance that burnished from deep within that only unqualified love could kindle and fuel. "He looked terrible when he came in. He whispered for me to call 911 as he grabbed his chest. I thought maybe this was a scary warning to change his lifestyle. Cut back on stress. He'd been so careful to exercise and watch his cholesterol and all. I felt so helpless and scared, watching him struggle for breath."

Melody could hardly bear any more of Marisa's painful discourse, but didn't want her to quit, either. She knew it was important for Marisa to talk.

"It seemed like eternity for the ambulance to get to here, then suddenly paramedics where everywhere. I hardly dared to breathe. I smiled at Grant, telling him over and over he was going to be all right.

"The paramedics were making strange invasive noises. Plastic packages being ripped open. Questions. Directions. Beeping machines. Hands everywhere at once on Grant's body. Then Grant smiled at me through all that. I was finally able to breathe again and returned his smile. I was sure he was going to be all right.

"Then I heard Eric's terrified little voice. 'Mom! Dad! What's happening? Mom?' Eric ran home from playing across the street when he heard the ambulance stop. He looked at his father surrounded by strangers doing strange things and he asked me if his daddy was dead in a tiny frightened whisper.

"I told him no. I reassured him Daddy was going to be okay. I guess I was trying to convince myself at the same time.

"The paramedics moved quickly to stabilize Grant and get him into the ambulance. I heard bits of voices and static responses over their radio as I got in the back. When I saw the faces of the paramedics who were still working on Grant, I was even more scared than before. I discovered there's no bottom to the pit of fear.

"When we arrived at the hospital emergency entrance, I gave Grant a kiss filled with hope and love. I squeezed the hand that didn't have a needle stuck into it, trying not to let him see how afraid I really was. Grant was wheeled into a room and activity seemed to magnify behind closed curtains. A nurse whisked me into a small empty waiting room where there was a phone. That's when I called you guys."

Melody remembered the rest of the day vividly. Minutes after answering the phone, she and Stuart were in the small private room with Marisa waiting for word on Grant's condition. Waiting. Waiting. And then the unthinkable. A total stranger, the emergency room doctor, came in with a defeated look on his face.

"I'm sorry, Mrs. Fisher. I'm so sorry. There was nothing we could do. He had a massive heart attack." Those were his exact words and they burned in Melody's memory along with Marisa's response.

"Oh, my god," Marisa had whispered in the smallest, saddest voice that flowed directly from her broken heart. "Oh my god!" she'd repeated in shock and grief. "Grant." Mournful, tear filled eyes pleadingly searched the faces of those in the room, begging for the words to be wrong — to undo the moment in time. "Oh my god," Marissa cried as Stuart and Melody together hugged her, holding her sobbing body, their own disbelieving tears unleashed in that same instant on that awful afternoon.

When Marisa finished recalling the previous Sunday, a sorrowful silence shrowded the Fisher house and hung in the room like a ruminent mist.

"I'm going to go upstairs and check on Eric and Josh. Okay?" Melody asked, breaking the trance-like quiet.

Marisa nodded numbly.

Seven year old Josh Fisher was sleeping fitfully. Melody leaned over him and gently kissed him on the cheek before going into Eric's room. She began reading the sleeping Eric his favorite story, more to comfort herself than for his well being. Melody read the end of the story in a broken whisper through silent sobs. She closed Eric's book and laid it on the floor by the sleeping child's bed. "It's not fair to lose your father at five years old," Melody choked. As she quietly left the sleeping child she gave him a soft, tender hug and stroked his hair. "Your mom has an awfully hard road ahead of her, and I promise you, I'll be there with her for your school plays and ball games—first girlfriend, first heartache, and the same for your brother. I'll be there whenever she needs me. Your mom is my dearest friend and always will be."

Melody Fox slowly, quietly got up off the edge of the bed Eric was sleeping in, and backed out of his room, never taking her eyes off his sweet sleeping face.

Still silent in the kitchen, Stuart looked at Marisa, his partner's widow, and tears once more caught in his eyes. Marisa put her hand on the back of Stuart's hand and tried to comfort him. The inconsolable comforting the inconsolable. No one wanted the evening to end, to accept that the world would continue without Grant Fisher. There was no stopping tomorrow and all the tomorrows to follow.

Marisa bravely broke the silence. "You guys go on home. I'll be all right. Actually, I'm exhausted. It's been a long, difficult day for all of us. Please. Go on home." Silent tears, again began gliding down her cheeks. She pulled out the very used tissue in her pocket, wiped her nose, and composed herself. Again. Marisa had made the exact same motions countless times over the past four days. "Thank you guys," she whispered and got up from the table. The three friends hugged, clinging to each other for comfort. Hesitantly they eased apart slightly, their foreheads still touching in an attempt to let go and hold on at the same time.

Melody and Stuart each kissed Marisa on the cheek, squeezed her hand, then sadly they left.

Marisa took the dirty coffee cups to the sink, leaned against the edge of the counter and cried. She searched for her soggy tissue and took a deep breath to gather strength. It was time to go upstairs. There was nothing left to do except go to bed in their queen size bed, with Grant's familiar scent still lingering faintly on the linens. She promised herself she would never, ever wash his pillow case, treasuring forever the nearness of him.

2

"Life goes on." Stuart's dispirited words escaped through his abysmal sadness as he and Melody walked toward their car. The plaintive phrase was picked up by the cool, dark night and carried off to infinity by the desert wind. "Damn." His voice quavered as he spit out the expletive. He opened the car door and silently slid behind the wheel as Melody got in on the passenger side. Stuart pounded the steering wheel with the palms of both hands in a mixture of heartache and anger. He looked sadly at Melody seated next to him as he started the car and slowly pulled away from the curb. "He was my partner. My friend. We balanced each other. He was like a brother to me."

Melody's sorrow for Grant was profound and pervasive while her concern for Stuart's seemingly fathomless grief was equally intense. "Grant was so exuberant—so full of life. Those poor little boys. I'll miss him so much. He was part of our life, Stu. I'm sure it'll be even harder for you with work and all." Instantly she wished once again, as she so often did, that she had more control over what impulsively came out of her mouth. She had intended to make his deep sorrow a little less painful. The words that came out would do just the opposite. Melody turned and looked out the side window. She noticed they weren't headed for home where she could get her hands on a couple of aspirins and a glass of water, lie down, close her eyes, and hopefully escape this staggering sadness with some dreamless sleep.

"Where're we going?" she asked, interrupting Stuart's solemnity.

"I don't have any idea. I just can't go home yet." Anguish punctuated his somberness, and Melody thought better of saying any more. They drove around Scottsdale and Phoenix for what seemed like hours in heavy-hearted silence. Down Scottsdale Road, past Stuart and Grant's office, across Bell Road, down Tatum, through the Papago mountains, round in circles with no place to escape from the reality of the last four awful days. Stuart's mixture of sorrow and anger showed on his face.

Melody knew his anger was neither directed toward her, caused by her, nor controlled by her, but she still felt that it was her responsibility to do something about it. She turned to look at her husband, still tortured, still driving nowhere. She really wanted him to unleash his grief, but she didn't want to sound like a psychologist either. He hated it when she brought her 'professional expertise' into their conversations, so she remained quiet. Not all that easy for Melody under the best of circumstances, let alone in the silence that filled every molecule in the car.

Finally, Melody recognized the familiar tall palms as they approached the entrance leading the few short blocks to the home they had just built. Their house was quiet and dark and emitted a sense of normalcy that contradicted their mood.

They were emotionally and physically drained. "I can't think about this any more. Let's just go to bed," Melody suggested, cracking the somber echo of their footfalls in the silence as they walked into the kitchen from the garage. "Come on." She took Stuart's hand. Impulsively, they embraced each other in the moonlit kitchen, clinging like magnets. Stuart finally wept on Melody's shoulder, smothering his sobs in the warmth of her neck, smelling her scent, grasping her thick, auburn hair in his hands, holding her like there might be no tomorrow.

Stuart restlessly tossed and turned in bed for hours until just before sunrise, his exhausted mind and body surrendered into a tormented, dream filled sleep. Morning came too soon. Friday. He managed his morning rituals and dressed in his favorite jacket and tie, grasping at any talisman that might help get him through the day.

Stuart forced himself to move one foot in front of the other, get behind the wheel of his car, put it in reverse, and back down the driveway. Go. Continue. Every movement was like wading through glue.

Nothing would be the same once he walked into the office. Grant would never again be sitting at his desk where they could schmooze and create and be brilliant together. Stuart was secretly, desperately afraid of being able to keep up the agency's work and reputation without Grant, but he didn't share that thought with Melody. The partners had had their spotlight of glory just a year ago when their commercial for liver flavored gourmet dog treats turned out to be the favorite commercial of the year, garnering them interviews on the *Today Show* and *David Letterman*, not to mention glowing accolades in *Advertising Age, Ad Week, Arizona Business Magazine,* and *The Arizona Republic.*

Melody, too, was experiencing more mental anguish going back to work after such a shocking loss than she'd expected she would. Going past the familiar Sonoran landscape she'd driven past a thousand times, she thought of Marisa starting life from this day forward as she had never expected it would be. Nothing's the same. Past the ancient Saguaro cactus that stood there for hundreds of years. Same Palo Verde trees. Same old Brittlebush. Same old hawks — well, maybe not the exact same old hawks — slowly gliding in mindless circles on air currents hundreds of feet up, silhouetted against the clear, blue sky with nothing on their minds.

Everything's the same.

Nothing's the same.

Melody felt as tangible as a shadow as she opened the door to her office. No spirit. No presence. She felt awkward, like wearing somebody else's shoes, worn soft in the wrong places and still stiff where they should be worn. Just entering her familiar office was disquieting. Disturbing. Unsettling. She sat down in her brown, worn leather chair behind her small oak desk. Nothing in her office seemed to fit her which hadn't mattered one iota before. Now she craved having objects reflect her.

Today would be arduous. Her heart wasn't in her work and Melody felt she would be cheating her patients, a concept that conflicted completely with her work ethic and her nature. She considered canceling all her appointments but a first day back at work had to happen sometime. Today might as well be it. She had two depressed middle aged women, one mother of a teenage son who was likely frying his brain on drugs, one panic disorder, and her new pro bono client to see before she could escape this ten by eleven foot box of an office and call it a day.

Just then her eyes were drawn to something quirky that didn't belong on her desk. There was a hand scrawled note sitting on top of the papers she'd left last Friday. The single word 'NEXT' was scrawled in childish looking handwriting. Melody was sure there was a plausible explanation. She was too booked to give it more thought, and stashed the note in her top right hand desk drawer until she had time to think about it.

"So, Gail, who's on first?" Melody asked the psychology group's receptionist after she'd poured herself a cup of black coffee and assumed her professional mantle.

"You have Sarah Small any minute now, then Gina Otero, then a new patient who could only come during lunch, so I went ahead and scheduled her. Her name's Molly McGinnis," Gail continued in her annoying, cloying, bright Friday morning voice that even on any other day was just as annoying. "I left you open from one 'till two for lunch. Then you just have Karen Studeman and that lady Social Services is sending over."

"She has a name, Gail," Melody reprimanded. She hated the lack of respect her co-workers had for the two pro bono clients they allowed her to see.

"Sorry," Gail replied flippantly as she looked at the appointment book again. "Janice Makowsky," Gail enunciated carefully in her irritating high pitch and self important manner. "And, uh, sorry about your friend's husband's dying like that. How awful." The condolence came from about as deep as her back teeth — certainly not from her heart. Melody had never been sure Gail actually had one.

"Thank you." The condolence brought another flood of sadness that remained barely under control. She quickly stuffed her personal feelings back into the appropriate cubby hole where they belonged, locked away until after she'd listened to and tended to other people's personal sagas of mental anguish. Then and only then could she legitimately allow her own personal emotions to surface.

A few weeks ago Melody's patient load, as well as her level of professional satisfaction, had been at an all time low so she'd called Social Services to volunteer to take on a couple of cases. Scottsdale had certainly been good to her and Stuart, and she was idealistic enough to want to give something back to the community she now called home. It made her feel vital to be providing help to someone who would likely progress into a debilitating decline without her professional help. The three other psychologists in the group called her naive for thinking that helping two pro bono clients would have any effect on the well being of society but she didn't care.

Jamie Duncan, Pam Brock, and Wendy Ives had worked hard to establish their practice as one that attracted a roster of profitable, paying patients. They had all paid their dues in free work years before Melody had met them so they understood her sophomoric burning desire to help the needy. They also knew that her optimism would likely not burn brighter over time, but burn out like most others in their field had. The homeless and hopeless masses of the world, or even Phoenix were not their focus anymore, but if Melody needed to experience that on her own, the practice could tolerate a few gratis patients once in a while.

Melody finished her paperwork on her last client of the morning, her new client—Poor Molly—as she personally thought of her. It was finally time for her late lunch break and Melody couldn't wait to get out of the office. She said goodbye to Gail and went out into the Scottsdale sunshine, into her car. She picked up a drive-through salad and headed for a quick, quiet, outside spot for an undisturbed lunch where she could stare at the mountains she so loved. She had less than an hour to refuel before her next patient.

Karen Studeman, her two o'clock, was doing remarkably well for someone plagued with panic attacks. With medication and continued sessions for another couple months, she would likely be able to function on a much more integrated level than she could just nine months ago. Melody was as proud of Karen's progress as if she'd made the journey back from agoraphobia herself. Keeping her professional distance was something Melody was always fighting to maintain.

"Janice Makowsky is here," Gail enunciated clearly and slowly, mocking Melody's reproach about her pro bono client from their earlier conversation.

"Thank you. I'll be right there." Melody was thankful this day was nearly over and that she'd managed not to think about Grant, Marisa, or Stuart for the past hour.

Janice Makowsky probably had been a nice looking woman at one time although she was rather unkempt now. She sat by herself across the room from the other waiting patients who looked at her insolently. Melody had to control her desire to snap at them "You realize any one of you could be in her shoes with only the slightest twist of fate." Actually, her disapproving, piercing eyes expressed her thoughts very clearly, and the three women patients of her office mates squirmed uncomfortably. She then pleasantly nodded her head in friendly greeting to the women she had just non-verbally chastised.

Janice Makowsky had recently been released from the state mental hospital into a group home where she was doing fairly well under medication and careful supervision. On the way down the hall toward Melody's office, Janice turned to look at Melody and abruptly spit out "I hate it there." And so the session began.

She needed to establish a bond with Janice Makowsky. Hmmm. Not a simple task when dealing with a paranoid schizophrenic whose diagnosis implicitly implied she trusted absolutely no one. It was an exhausting session, but encouraging. Melody believed she could help Janice Makowsky. As long as Janice continued taking her medication and got continuous counseling, she just might make it.

Yes! This is more like it! This is what it's all about, Melody thought as she ushered Janice out her door to see Gail to schedule another appointment. The pro bono work was going to be a continuous part of her practice no matter what she had to do to continue it.

She made a new file for Janice Makowsky, wrote down her notes and comments, and was ready to call it a day. Melody was drained and stimulated at the same time.

This Friday had dragged fretfully slowly, even though she'd been busy non-stop. Her enthusiasm for her present position as lowest-on-the-totem-pole psychologist in an upscale small private practice in Scottsdale was eroding faster than a beach in a hurricane. Indeed, she had helped many women lead much happier and productive lives, but felt a lot more useful counseling her two non-paying social services appointees.

There was an uncomfortable, undirected niggling and gnawing at Melody while she drove the familiar route home in her red Jeep Cherokee. It was destroying her routine drive time decompression session and she wanted the feeling to go away. It was as if she'd forgotten her purse or she'd forgotten a lunch appointment or some crucial event but she couldn't manage to remember whatever it was that had been left undone. As she was forced to stop abruptly at a yellow light she'd been sure the car ahead of her would drive through, the jerk of her car and screeching tires dislodged the misplaced thought buried in her brain.

It was the note she'd stuffed in the drawer in her office. NEXT. Next what, she thought. Who's next? Next after what? What was first? There were enough off balance people coming in and out of the practice that any number of people could have left the note for any number of countless deranged reasons. Maybe it wasn't even meant for her.

Ever since she was quite young, Melody had an innate ability to easily put aside things that other people would stew about. Or maybe call the police about. She lived a simple, safe, boring life.

3

There was absolutely nothing—nothing—that caused Stuart Fox as much grief, panic, depression, and terror than thoughts of growing old. Not even the contemplation of dying was as horrendous as visions of getting old and weary. Aging was cruel, disgusting, and ugly. Aches and pains, labored breathing, atrophied muscles, sagging skin, and loss of hearing, mobility, and memory. Add to those miserable prospects the increased likelihood of cancer, Alzheimers, arthritis, and heart disease, and you have Stuart's view of aging.

Stuart had been nearly obsessed with thoughts of the degenerative, disabling effects of aging to a degree bordering on fanatical since his thirtieth birthday. Melody had tried repeatedly and unsuccessfully to assure him that the Grim Reaper was most likely more than a blink away. He scowled at wisecracking birthday cards and bristled at jokes about aging. Wisdom, he'd been assured, was the trade off that came with maturity. Ha! Wisdom — it seemed a minuscule compensation for everything that aging took away.

Reaching forty had hit Stuart exceptionally hard. The image that his past was as long—or possibly longer—than his future made him miserable. Being able to remember thirty years back was chilling. His mid-life crisis had been stinging and substantive, rather than overt and fleeting. That's when he'd first begun privately surfing the internet for sites revealing discoveries and products that were purported to extend life. Most of what he found was confusing, conflicting and downright bogus. He bought a few advertised, guaranteed remedies, but none made him feel or look any younger. Nothing he tried gave him any hope of living to a healthy one hundred five, his arbitrarily designated satisfactory end date, though he was still avidly searching.

Now he was forty two years old. Forty two and a half, going on forty three. Nearing fifty. A mindboggling half century. Most of Stuart's cohorts didn't consider forty two old, but in Stuart's designated play book, forty two was the beginning of a new era. Old age.

Stuart's doctor had really pissed him off at his last annual physical by responding to Stuart's serious question regarding the best means to avoid aging by answering with a flip retort: "The best way to live long is to have old parents." The doctor laughed at his own stale joke. "Short of that," he'd added, "watch what you eat, eliminate stress, exercise, don't smoke, and enjoy every day." Right.

Stuart vividly remembered thinking his father was old at forty, when Stuart was nine. Stuart's father had survived a first heart attack at forty nine, then died suddenly at fifty eight. "Sixteen years older than I am now. Sixteen years is nothing."

"I don't want to go last," Melody stated during one of their numerous provocative 'discussions' regarding whether it was preferable to live a full life no matter how short, or live a long life, no matter how impaired. "I don't want to be the one going to funerals for everybody I've known and loved, lose them all, and then be the last remaining relic of my generation. And I don't want to outlive whatever money I've saved and have to eat dog food or be a bag lady or dependent on our children who by then would be tired of the burden of taking care of us."

"I sure as hell don't want to die young, damn it. I don't want to die! I want live long and be strong and vibrant and mentally alert."

Stuart repeatedly railed that you should be entitled to a long, healthy life. Melody wondered where he'd found those rules.

"Well, sure. You and everybody else. Seriously, Stuart, when I get old and sick I don't want tubes leading in and out of every orifice of my body keeping me alive. When I'm old and feeble, let me go."

Stuart looked lovingly at Melody. "Don't get old and feeble," Stuart begged sincerely, real trepidation apparent in his expression as he tenderly traced her face with his fingertips.

"I'll do my damnedest, but it happens. Getting old happens if you're lucky. I can only hope one day I'll be old, sitting in a chair in the sun, reflecting back on a wonderful life, a loving family, and a handful of great grandchildren whose names I probably won't be able to keep straight." Age wasn't an issue for Melody. Maybe because she was only thirty five. Starting a family—that was her greatest, most timely concern.

To appease Stuart's irrational craving for a long, healthy life, Stuart and Melody's house included an entire room specifically designed as a home gym—low pile carpet, extra air conditioning vents, a full mirrored wall, and a substantial amount of exercise equipment that was dusted more often than used. Once in a while Stuart would become zealous about using it, but that usually lasted between four to ten days, depending where the weekend fell within his spirit of best intentions. He didn't golf or play tennis, although he often thought about taking up both. They were good for your health, but the time involved in any sport was always a deterrent to actually doing it. After sixty hour plus work weeks, Stuart didn't have the drive to go hit and chase golf balls or tennis balls. Occasionally, he'd go on a bike ride with Melody, but it was a rare occurrence. Hiking had never tripped his trigger. Certainly not fishing, which Stuart never saw as exercise anyway. Jogging sounded like the ideal exercise until he tried it. But his knees couldn't take it. Sport for the sake of exercise just didn't make sense to him.

Stuart was acutely aware that the young guys and sharp women entering advertising were now approaching half his age—more savvy about computer technology and the latest in special effects than he was. More in tune with the Generation Xers than he was. Stuart wouldn't even be in the media buyers' prized eighteen to forty nine year old demographic age group much longer. He was now closing in on the fifty to sixty four year old age group in terms of marketers targeting their products—prescription drugs, hair dyes, estate planning, retirement homes—old people products.

Stephanie Zoller walked solemnly into Stuart's office, working hard at keeping herself from tears. She held a mug of coffee in each hand and gave one to Stuart. "I miss him," Stephanie stated flatly. She had been Grant's administrative assistant for the past six years.

"I do too, Stephanie." Then, with a gulp of coffee and a deep sigh, Stuart continued in a very strong, comforting, controlled voice. "I'm going to need your help sorting out what Grant was working on, what's due now, what was due last week, who's who, and what's what with his clients." Just last Friday—one short week ago Grant was working at his desk next door and the world had been normal.

Stephanie silently shook her head in acknowledgment, then, with a sigh, she began to recount the agency's activities from the previous Monday through Thursday. "We've canceled everything or taken care of what we could. Julie in media had a nightmare of a time, but she took care of everything that needed immediate attention. I assured her you'd approve, so if there's any problem, blame me. Here are the changes," she said as she handed Stuart a pile of papers. "I didn't want to disturb you. I canceled the talent and TV production for the Burgermeister commercial that was scheduled for today. They said for you to get in touch with them as soon as you can to reschedule. The campaign was supposed to break this coming Wednesday starting with the ten o'clock news—all three affiliates plus five cable stations—but

I was able to convince the Burgermeister people to push it back. I told them you'd try to get everything going within a week of the original dates. Will that work?" she continued without stopping to wait for an answer. "Radio's all okay. We've been able to rerun most newspaper ads without any trouble, but the tourism magazine ad couldn't wait. Four color, full page bleed. It's due by the end of today. I'll have Randy show you what he's got for them. I think you'll like it. We had to go ahead and have the client approve Randy's artwork and have films made." Stephanie made a slight, uncontrolled grimace — her eyebrows raising up, and her bottom lip stretching tight across her lower teeth that showed how worried she was for having made decisions she'd never made before. "Let's see. What else?" she continued. "You got a ton of cards, donations, and some flowers. There's a pile of checks to be signed." She nodded toward a pile consisting of checks and invoices on the left hand side of Stuart's desk. "Oh, Grant's new client, the Scottsdale Anti-Aging Clinic, they've called repeatedly but wouldn't leave any messages except for you to call as soon as possible. They wanted me to give them your home number, but I wouldn't. Grant said they'll probably be our biggest client once they get rolling."

Stuart listened to Stephanie's growing list of urgencies on top of his own stack of urgent and due yesterday piles. He and Grant had been the perfect team. Grant the more outgoing and business oriented partner, Stuart the more creative half. He had no idea how he'd handle the increased amount of work and responsibility that was now his alone. He didn't want to be caught up in administrative crap all day every day, but neither did he have anyone to delegate it to now.

As Stephanie walked out of Stuart's office, he picked up his coffee and followed her into the hall for a moment. He walked over to Grant's office and leaned against the door jamb, sadly looking in at the quiet, organized emptiness there. He hadn't yet been able to bring himself to cross the threshold.

Standing in the doorway, strongly feeling Grant's presence,

Stuart suddenly and vividly remembered the dream that had tortured his sleep the previous night. The memory of it sucked the wind out of him and nearly buckled his knees. He had dreamt about Grant, young and virile, healthy and vibrant climbing a very steep rocky mountain. Stuart was at the bottom, looking up at him, watching him, afraid for him. "Be careful," Stuart cried out. Grant was having the time of his life.

"Whee-ooo," he heard Grant shout. "Come on, get up here Stu! It's incredible, man! What're you waiting for? You afraid? You an old man already!" Grant taunted. "This is exhilarating! It's intoxicating! Come on. You don't know what you're missing."

Stuart was anxious to get moving, get up there and feel the joy and elation of climbing higher and higher with Grant. He took a step forward, ready to run and jump, but his right foot staggered, slowly followed by the unsteady shuffle of his left foot. Stuart spied his own reflection in a shiny, mirror-like boulder at the bottom of the mountain and was shocked by the image he saw. He was old, wrinkled, and bent over. His eyes were small and squinty. His eyebrows white and bushy. His hair was thin and gray. He looked down and saw his hands were gnarled, his arthritic fingers grasping the top of a cane. His hips hurt just standing still. His back ached. It took so much strength just to take those two steps, Stuart knew he would never, ever climb that mountain. He would never again experience the rousing freedom and joy of accomplishing something physically stimulating and challenging that young men took for granted.

While standing a couple hundred feet from the mountain Stuart watched Grant who would always be young climb higher and higher. Grant's exclamations of glory punctuated Stuart's shocked survey of his wracked, unfamiliarly aged body. He could feel the freedom and powerful spiritual majesty of the climb but he couldn't move. It really didn't matter because he was too old, crippled, and weary to go forward more than a few steps. His heart wanted to soar to the top of the mountain, but his body was drained, exhausted, worn out. His mind was slow to respond. He was confused. How did Grant expect him to get up there?

Then, inexplicably he was himself again. Same age as Grant. Relief poured over him. Nothing was holding him back. He took off like a lion, newly freed from captivity. He sprinted across the rocky ground separating him from the base of the mountain and started climbing to reach Grant, loose rocks falling from his foot holds. It didn't matter. He was climbing — rushing, racing, rocketing to get to Grant who was still far ahead, his laughter rippling and echoing off the mountain, surrounding and encouraging Stuart to keep going. "Come on, Stuart."

Then Grant was gone, and Stuart was alone with no sound but howling wind. It was getting dark, the source of light having disappeared with Grant. Stuart was old once again. Not only was he incapacitated with painful arthritis, he was weak and frail. His clothes were old and worn and he was desperately cold. His vision was blurred and his breathing was labored. His hands shook with palsy. He was old and helplessly alone on the side of a mountain. He curled up on a flat ledge protected by an overhang of rock. Too frail to get up or down the mountain, he had no choice but to stay there in the dark and cold, and wait for someone else to come along and help him. He was absolutely incapable. And miserable.

"Stuart, there's a call for you on line three. It's Greg Parker," Stephanie said interrupting Stuart's tortured thoughts.

He was drenched in cold sweat and disoriented for a fraction of a second while reality took over from his fantasy. "Stuart?" he heard Stephanie again and willed himself back to the here and now. He looked at his hands — turned them palm side up then turned them again and looked at the backs. No gnarled arthritis. No old age spots. He was relieved. There were real problems to solve. Life goes on, Stuart repeated to himself again as he had been reciting daily, unconsciously.

"Who?"

"Greg Parker. Scottsdale Anti-Aging Clinic. Marketing Director."

How timely. If this clinic had any real methods of delaying or suspending the aging process, it would be the miracle Stuart was looking for. He thought most anti-aging plans were no more than scams for the distributors but was ever hopeful that he would find the real thing before it was too late. Anything was better than his inherited propensity for an early heart attack and the constant fear that went with it—along with his uncontrollable fears of losing his vitality and virility, memory, and mobility.

"Put him through," Stuart said as he walked into his own office and swiveled around in his high-backed black leather chair. "That's the client Laurel told Grant about but hasn't amounted to much yet, right?" Stuart asked before picking up the phone. Stephanie was visibly put off balance at Stuart's harsh tone regarding Grant's success at getting a potentially huge account. Stephanie nodded affirmatively.

"Hi, Greg. This is Stuart."

"Hi Stuart. Ahh, first I want to say how sincerely sorry we were to hear about Grant. It was such a shock to all of us here. We'd just had lunch together last Friday and he was fine. I can only imagine how hard it's been for you. My sincere condolences..."

"Thank you," Stuart interrupted. Greg just kept going.

"...and I hate to be crass and intrude on your mourning, but business is business and we do need to continue on this work Grant started. I'll be up front and honest, we have to be sure we'll get the same quality work out of your agency that we were getting before."

Was he setting Stuart up so they could get rid of Fisher and Fox? Or was Stuart just becoming paranoid?

"Will you personally be handling us now, or will someone else within your agency be taking over? I'll be honest, we specifically told Grant we want to work with the principals on this. It's..."

That's twice he's used the word honest. It was difficult to

interpret the nuances of meaning behind the statement, not having personally met Greg Parker, the person attached to the other end of the phone voice he was listening to.

"I'm looking forward to it," Stuart interjected enthusiastically, dredging up the confident tone from somewhere unknown to him.

"Good. Then we really need to get going immediately, at least on finalizing our logo, stationary, and the whole corporate image package," continued Greg. "Both the interior and exterior signage need to be approved yesterday to stay on schedule and we don't even have our logo pinned down yet. What's your schedule like this afternoon?"

Pushy little twerp, was the first mental picture that came to Stuart's mind. "Anytime's fine. I'll make the time to fit your schedule. I'm looking forward to meeting you and I also want to get moving on your account immediately. I need a little time to look over Grant's files and preliminary work before we meet so we're all on the same page here. You're an important client to us, and I appreciate your faith in our agency." To us. Our agency. Oh my god. Stuart realized with profound sadness and a pinch of fear that our agency wasn't accurate anymore.

His calendar was full but he would have to have his assistant, Annie, clear some time.

"Late afternoon's fine."

"Good. We'll give you a complete tour, introduce everybody, and then we can get you up to date. You know where we are?"

"Yep. I pass your building every day."

"I want to make sure Clark Shepard, our medical director, is available and Eva Blackwell, too. She's part owner and our lead research person, and of course I want you to meet Jeff McGonagle, the CEO while you're here, but he's always here. You'll be working with me mostly, but Clark and Eva will have a lot of information you'll need. It's better to get it first hand rather than from me. See you later. How 'bout four." It wasn't a question.

"Four o'clock, then."

"Thanks, Stuart. I look forward to meeting you."

As soon as he hung up, Annie buzzed with another call from another major client. He was kept on the phone right up until time to leave for his appointment with the clinic. Lots of condolences. Lots of clients to reassure that the agency would still produce the same high quality work. Stuart could be very convincing. It was easy to reassure their clients. It was himself he was having a hard time convincing.

4

Stuart looked at the sticky note Stephanie had attached to his jacket sleeve on the way out of the office with the names of the people he'd be meeting. Greg Parker, marketing director, the twerp Stuart would spend most of his time with, Dr. Clark Shepherd, medical director, Eva Blackwell, the research director, and Jeff McGonagle, CEO.

Stuart headed north on Scottsdale Road as he did routinely on his way home. The clinic was on the east side of the street, set back about four hundred feet. He'd watched as it was being built over the last several months. He had first assumed it was another golf club or spa resort until Grant told him what it was and that they had a real chance of getting the account from the ground up.

The Scottsdale Anti-Aging Clinic was a sweeping, grand scale, contemporary Pueblo style building constructed of curvaceous tan adobe. The north and south wings were architecturally balanced sections of various heights so they appeared to be an Indian pueblo. No roof line was less than an imposing twelve feet tall with flat roofs and canales from which the infrequent rain would drain. There were tall narrow windows facing west with larger broad windows to the north and south. The main entrance soared eighteen feet high where a portico supported by cantera stone columns defined broad archways. The grounds in front of the building were meticulously landscaped in ornamental grasses, native shrubs, palms, cactus and red rock. In the middle of the front of the five acre property was a peaceful pond edged in stone with a classical three tiered Spanish fountain in the middle and a dozen or more individual jets spitting water in graceful arches. "If it isn't the fuckin' fountain of youth." Stuart exclaimed to himself.

The approach from the road to the clinic wound around the pond. The front doorway was flanked with large potted cactus and flowering plants. The front double doors were carved wood, ten feet tall, with huge bronze knobs cast in the shape of cactus flowers.

Stuart couldn't hold back a whistle as he parked his car in the space marked visitor and got out, glad no one was there to observe his amazement at the splendor and craftsmanship of the building. Normally Stuart was not impressed with magnificence or grand scale anything. The Scottsdale Anti-Aging Clinic however surpassed 'superb' by his own unattainable high standard of excellence. Stepping inside the foyer the first thing he noticed was a curved reception desk of honed sandstone. Very tasteful. The patina on all the walls and ceiling were finished in the same mottled earth tones as the stone desk.

This is my kind of place, Stuart murmured to himself. As a seasoned marketing maven he knew that was exactly the response this clinic intended to elicit from their upscale clientele. Nothing was more comforting, nothing did a better job of creating immediate confidence than walking into a 'my-kind-of-place' establishment when about to spend big bucks. And Stuart could smell big bucks everywhere, from the stone floor to the immense wrought iron chandelier hanging from the ceiling, to the posh receptionist at the desk.

"Stuart Fox," the receptionist stated knowingly as she got up from behind the desk and floated over to shake hands with Stuart. She continued in her well modulated, refined voice void of any regional accent whatsoever, "You're here to see Greg." She was dressed in a cobalt blue suit—not too conservative, not too bold. "I'm Mandy Johnson. Nice to meet you. Greg'll be here in a minute. Can I get you some coffee, iced tea, or water?"

"Water would be great. Thanks."

"Have a seat. I'll be right back."

Stuart took a seat in one of the kilim upholstered chairs near Mandy's desk. His recurrent fear about the financial viability of every new account nearly disappeared.

He heard the soft sound of men's leather soled shoes on the stone floor before he saw anyone. A pleasant looking man with an engaging smile who appeared to be quite young—younger than Stuart, taller than Stuart, and thinner, too—approached him just as Mandy returned from his left with an opened bottle of water and a glass. A glass glass with a stem. Not plastic. Stuart got up, thanked Mandy, then had no free hand to shake with the person briskly walking toward him who must be Parker. Greg Parker was no twerp.

Greg was at least six feet four, dressed in an Italian suit and expensive Italian shoes. He had a hair cut that probably cost as much as dinner for eight in an average restaurant. "Hello Stuart." Greg greeted Stuart with an outstretched hand which he nonchalantly began to withdraw as he saw Stuart juggling the bottle and glass.

Stuart managed to free his right hand, only spilling a drop of bottled water and shook hands. "Greg. This is quite a place. I thought it was a country club while it was being built."

Greg smiled knowingly. "Thanks. That's just the response we'd hoped for. Come on, I'll take you on a tour," Greg continued in his deep engaging voice as he turned to the right, placed a big hand on Stuart's back and guided him in the direction of the office he had just come out of. "Why don't you leave your briefcase in my office and we'll get started."

Greg's office was in the south wing facing east with expansive windows overlooking the mountains. It was a very masculine space with a glove leather chair, black leather desk accessories on a large polished wooden desk, a book case filled with books and a number of framed family snapshots, and two rich gray upholstered chairs facing the desk. "These are all administrative offices in the south wing," Greg announced as they started down the stone hall. There's Jeff's office at the end, next to his office is Sawyer Wiles' office. He's our chief financial officer. Smart guy. We're lucky to have him on board. Next is Clark's office, medical director. He's a native of Scottsdale. Don't find too many of them around here. This one's Diane's office. She's our nutritionist."

Since the door was open, Greg stepped in to say hello. "Hi, Diane. Meet Stuart Fox from Fisher and Fox."

"Hi," she responded with a smile. Stuart nodded, imagining she could tell immediately that he was a voracious meat eater which she probably scorned.

"Connor Nelson. He's our board certified physologist, our muscle man. Alice Winters' office. She's our plastic surgeon. She's one of our part time docs. We also have a part time rheumatologist and dermatologist. They're each here one day a week. Across the hall are our administrative assistants, and I'll spare you the names and introductions for now. You'll get to know them all later. Next is Moselle Bleu. She's a psychiatrist with a dual specialty in geriatrics and neuropharmacology.

"We'll go on down this hall to the lab area." Greg pushed open the big wooden door. "Here's Eva's office. She's our Research and Lab Director — a molecular biologist. She's coming to our meeting after the tour and you'll meet her then."

The lab was sparkling with glass and stainless steel. "We'll be doing some work in conjunction with the National Institutes of Health and Arizona State University. Eva and her staff got us the government grants to get us going. It's all very exciting. Her assistant isn't here today, but you'll probably meet her before too long. It's astonishing what we've learned about the quote disease," he emphasized wiggling two fingers of each hand in the air, "of aging."

There were few idiosyncrasies that annoyed Stuart more than making hand quotation marks in the air. He hoped his cringe was subdued enough to go unnoticed.

"We'll give you some info on it. One of your first assignments for us is going to be to do a brochure about aging as a disease anyway. When you're done, you'll know more than you ever knew existed in the area of geriatrics and this new field — anti-aging."

"Good. I've already learned more than I care to know about dogs' digestive systems, garage doors, and way more than I wanted to know about fast food hamburgers. Personally, I find the area of aging — anti-aging — extremely intriguing."

Greg smiled the pleased grin of an evangelist converting another to his flock and led Stuart to a large door opening to a covered portale around the back of the clinic. "Let's go back this way."

They went outside and walked across the wide stone patio that faced the mountains. All the executive offices had windows that captured the resplendent McDowell Mountain view. The back of the clinic grounds stretched out even farther than the front. The large flagstone patio was surrounded by huge reddish brown boulders defining the edge of the graceful space. There were wooden tables and chairs with green market umbrellas opened in the center of each table, and brilliant potted flowers everywhere — on the tables, between the tables, and in between the boulders.

"We often have lunch out here. It's my favorite space in the whole complex," Greg said as he kept walking. "Just beyond the patio you can see some equipment. It's part of Connor's department. Clients learn how to use this stuff here, and then they either get equipment at home, or come here regularly like a fitness club. There's also a pool over there. Not very deep. It's just for swimming laps. Then there's a heated, smaller pool for people with arthritis to start their workouts. We'll keep that at around ninety-five degrees once we get started."

Stuart was silent, nearly overwhelmed with their setup. "Can I live here?" he asked Greg.

"You may feel like you live here once we get things rolling. There's a lot of work to be done on your end, and it's all urgent at this point."

"I can't wait." Stuart thought that sounded desperate which was not at all what he meant. On second thought he realized he was close to desperate to get some income from this place. The clinic was either very well funded or in debt past their eyeballs. He had to find out, diplomatically, and soon, but not yet. The timing had to be proper or the question could be construed as a lack of faith, which doesn't create the best foundation for a solid relationship between client and agency. Nothing in Grant's notes had indicated how financially solid the clinic was. As the clinic's agency of record, Fisher and Fox would be responsible for all bills incurred by the clinic for their print pieces, magazine ad placements, broadcast production and air time. Everything that went through the agency ended up being their financial responsibility. An under-financed startup business was a bad risk.

When they reached the reception area again, this time from the outside, Greg opened the large glass doors and motioned with his head for Stuart to follow him.

"Down this way. In the north wing, we have examining rooms, the nurses station, another small lab just for urinalysis, blood work and stuff other than research, a physical therapy room, and an x-ray room. We don't have x-ray equipment yet. We'll start off referring clients to other radiology labs, but we may get our own equipment and radiologist later. Don't know yet. Originally we were going to have our own, but it came out to be financially inefficient."

So, thought Stuart, they're conscious of limitations, at least. "It looks like you didn't leave anything else out." Okay, ask now, Stuart thought to himself, but still held back. His curiosity was raging, but his professional judgment strangled him into silence. Timing is everything.

"We have plans for expansion in the future—an outpatient

surgery center, and possibly a hotel and spa like you thought from the beginning. Once we get going we expect to have clients from all over the world and they'll need a place to stay. There's a private airport near-by for those who want to fly in. Or, maybe someday we'll have a private plane to pick up and deliver our patients. Whatever we can do to make money.

"Oh, the kitchen. It's right here. What can I say. It's a kitchen. It's Diane's domain. Actually, it's a very important part of the total anti-aging process. We'll go into more of that later. Come on back to my office. I'll have Mandy call Eva and Clark and tell them we're ready, unless there's anything else you'd like to see."

Stuart shook his head no, although he could hardly refrain from asking Greg to show him the money. "This is simply a fantastic facility."

Stuart silently wondered how many extra years the clinic could give him. How long could they extend his life?

There were three people waiting for them in Greg's office. Stuart was expecting Clark Shepard and Eva Blackwell and had forgotten who else he was meeting. Stuart was awful at remembering names but excellent at remembering faces. He recognized all four as some of the unknown faces at Grant's funeral.

"Oh, Jeff, I'm glad you're here," Greg mentioned to one of the two men. "I'd like you all to meet Stuart Fox of Fisher and Fox Advertising Agency. This is Jeff McGonagle, CEO. Clark Shepard, medical director. Eva Blackwell, research and lab director." Stuart nodded and shook hands with each one as they were introduced.

Stuart's impression of the organization as he got to know more and more about it, continued to delight him. Unless something radical had happened to his ability to make accurate judgments on first impressions, this was going to be a highly gratifying group to work with. The CEO offered his condolences, made a few friendly, introductory remarks, and excused himself to get back to his office. Understandably, the CEO would have been anxious to eyeball Stuart and make his own judgment about the ability of this absolute stranger they were about to trust with a few hundred thousand dollars and the viability of their immediate as well as long term success.

Greg asked Clark Shepard to be the first to explain a little about the medical aspect of anti-aging medicine. Before he even opened his mouth, it was obvious the medical director liked talking about the subject. His back straightened slightly and he leaned forward in his chair. His eyes lit up like a kid who just ran home the winning score in a little league game, and he began an enthusiastic monologue. "We've known there are a lot of factors that affect aging in humans but until recently we didn't know how to control or manipulate these factors," Dr. Shepard began. Stuart wondered who he meant by 'we' but didn't interrupt. "A lot of aging is genetic. Gene p21 controls cell divisions as we grow old, and tweaking that gene is going to have a lot to do with how long people will be living. It'll have an effect on preventing diseases of old age and one hundred ten year olds will be commonplace. But we're not there yet. If everything goes as planned, we may be able to look forward to being in that healthy one hundred ten year old group. Certainly our children's generation can expect to live that long. 'Course p21 isn't the only factor that determines how long we live. How well you take care of yourself nutritionally and physically has a substantial impact. Taking supplements, not smoking, eating less fats and more foods rich in antioxidants, exercising regularly, staying out of the sun, all that stuff. You know, just a hundred years ago the average male life expectancy was around forty two."

Stuart's heart leaped into his throat, pounded in his ears, and then nearly stopped altogether at the statistic he just heard. His mind froze on those prodigious words. Forty two!

"And now, due to better nutrition and better medical care, people live to be around eighty three once they make it past sixty — unless they get hit by a truck or killed by a crazed spouse. We now know the number of times a cell can regenerate is a finite number that's imprinted within our cells. That's Eva's department, and she'll get into that more. The human body ages just like rusty iron, starting at around thirty. Regular, everyday bodily functions generate free radicals — molecules with an unpaired electron. Our bodies routinely eliminate these free radicals with antioxidants that are constantly produced by our cells. When you don't produce enough antioxidants, which happens, again, around thirty — zip — the free radicals steal an electron from some other molecule which then needs an electron and a whole domino effect happens. You can thankfully increase your antioxidant levels through vitamins C and E, and other supplements. You can also replace hormones to replicate younger stages in life — DHEA, human growth hormones — stuff like that.

"So physically, here at our clinic, first we check the overall well being of a patient with a complete physical. We check blood and urine for levels of free radicals, antioxidants, hormone levels, and so forth and then prescribe whatever each individual's needs are to restore them to a younger, healthier state. Patients have to be monitored regularly to make sure their levels are correct. Sometimes supplemental antioxidant intake can keep normal cells from producing what they've regularly produced, and that sets up a dependency without any benefit. Well, that's sure counterproductive, so of course, we'd need to alter the dosage. Playing with hormones, especially human growth hormones, is something that has to be very carefully monitored. Hormones have lots of different effects. You don't want to create negative hormonal reactions."

Greg broke in, putting an end to Clark's recitative. "We also know, as I'm sure you do, being in advertising, that physical appearance is an important value in our Western culture — like it or not. It's not a secret that good looking kids get more attention in schools, better looking people get hired faster, and tall people often get more respect than short people. It's just awful, but it's 'the American way' and there's no sense denying it." Stuart bit his lip when Greg made air quotation marks again. "So, we work with patients to make the absolute best of their physical appearance as well as their physical state. When you look good, you feel good—that's a given. Sometimes all it takes is a small change. Sometimes it's more of a challenge, shall we say. We have a plastic surgeon who does face lifts, hair transplants, liposuction, and other cosmetic surgery. We have a dermatologist who does micro-dermabraision to resurface skin from sun damage, acne scars, broken capillaries, scars, and some line and wrinkle removal. We can take ten years off, easily. But staying young is another issue. And that's Eva's department."

Stuart recognized Eva as the woman in the purple suit from Grant's funeral. Stuart could readily see Eva was bored with both Clark Shepard and Greg Parker. She didn't even attempt to hide it. She seemed to be a no-nonsense woman with little tolerance for anything other than her realm of expertise. On the other hand, maybe she was simply annoyed because she really didn't have time to sit there listening to information she already knew. Whatever the case, Stuart thought she was rude, and on top of that a smug superiority complex surrounded her.

"Here's the most exciting part," Eva began, obviously putting Dr. Shepard's presentation down, and giving strength to Stuart's original observation that she was highly educated but still ill-mannered. "Basically, human cells are designed to die off and replace themselves over and over again. Now we've discovered the likelihood that there's a genetically imprinted finite number of times a cell can replace itself." She spoke slowly and deliberately as if Stuart was a third grader getting into something over his head.

"As the replacement process slows down, which it does with age, the body loses it's ability to fight off diseases and generally weakens. Researchers I've worked with have found an enzyme called telomerase produced by cells on the ends of chromosomes. As telomeres shorten, cells stop reproducing themselves at the rate they did when they were younger. Some of them, pfffft, just can't anymore," she emphasized by flinging her right hand backwards. "So, there's actually a pretty simple equation for staying young: Keep those telomeres at the tails of chromosomes from dissolving. The only negative part is, we don't know how to keep them from dissolving yet. Not in people, anyway, but we're close.

"Of course there are always risks involved in playing around with cell division. Cancer is the result of uncontrolled division of certain cells. So some people think by manipulating this enzyme it's possible to cause human cells to divide uncontrollably and turn healthy cells into malignant cells. That's garbage of course. Studies and experiments at the University of Texas have found they don't. In fact, in Texas they're researching telomerase as a possible way to treat cancer.

"We have grant money to study the current longevity of various cells, especially liver, blood, and brain cells and also to conduct experiments with extending the natural life span of cells in worms and rats. We've just recently started that. We're involved with Ph.D. students at Arizona State who'll be doing their lab work here."

At the end of her commentary, Eva and Clark excused themselves to get back to their offices. Greg and Stuart were left alone to discuss marketing goals and advertising objectives.

"Anti-aging medicine's been accepted in Europe for years, but not here. We expect to change that and your responsibility will be to make that happen."

Stuart had a premonition of great things to come from this account—personally and professionally. He enjoyed Greg, other than his infrequent annoying mannerisms, and believed this could indeed be his chance to create the campaign that would make a huge success of the Scottsdale Anti-Aging Clinic, not to mention significantly increase the prosperity of Fisher and Fox Advertising Agency. Whether it was fate, luck, or coincidence that brought Stuart to this place instead of Grant, Stuart was so grateful he was feeling guilty.

Stuart left after seven, inspired and exhausted. He couldn't wait to talk to Melody, although he knew there was the strong possibility she would think this whole anti-aging thing was a bunch of high priced crap.

There was so much Stuart hadn't done in his life yet. How much time did he have? How many cell divisions were left for him? Stuart most desperately wanted his cells to keep dividing for at least another sixty years.

Of all the things he'd heard and learned, the one phrase incessantly replaying in his head was 'average life expectancy was around forty two.' Stuart was exactly forty two. If he'd been born a hundred years ago, he'd be dead now. He laughed at the stupidity of the statement, then the sobering thought of Grant dead at forty two gave him an icy chill.

5

There were more details that needed taking care of for the Scottsdale Anti-Aging Clinic's grand opening than an entire staff of event planners could do in the short time available, yet Stuart delegated very little in the way of details and decisions. He felt compelled to do the job alone or in some way he'd be letting Grant down. Everything else in his life was forced to take a back seat to the preparations for the gala grand opening of the Scottsdale Anti-Aging Clinic.

Now, it was show time.

Invitations had been sent to local and regional business leaders — especially those with CEO's over the age of forty. Every network affiliate, cable company, radio station, newspaper, and magazine publisher in Arizona was invited as well as Democratic and Republican legislators in Arizona, New Mexico, Texas, and California if they were even remotely involved in healthcare administration or costs. Medical directors, doctors, and insurance company managers had all been personally invited and were beginning to arrive. Some of the actors and celebrities living in the Phoenix area who were also on the invitation-only list to this gala opening could be spotted at the bar. All Fisher and Fox clients had been issued invitations, plus Stuart personally called every client to invite them to the opening. He'd recently lost a big account due, they said, to insufficient attention to their account. Stuart didn't believe they'd been slighted and worried what their real reason might have been, but he was stretched too thin to do anything about it.

There were three objectives that Stuart and Greg Parker had identified for this evening's gala. One was to inform the public of the viability of anti-aging medicine as a bona fide medical specialty, not some hocus pocus contemporary version of Wild West pitchmen's elixirs in a splashy twenty first century package. Information from the American Academy of Anti-Aging Medicine was included in the media kits prepared for print and broadcast representatives and available to everyone in attendance. Secondly, they wanted to immediately establish the clinic as the premier regional facility in this specialty field, keeping any other organization from considering competing for a share of the lucrative southwest market. Strike preemptively and keep the competition out. And third was to have prospective clients, especially influential people, calling first thing in the morning making appointments to start their personal anti-aging process so they would tell others how outstanding the clinic's program was. And of course, get some cash flowing into the business.

Lavish fresh flower arrangements were everywhere, a string quartet played outside on the patio and a pianist performed inside. Everything was set for a memorable, first class event that would be talked about throughout Phoenix, and would hopefully also earn a priceless amount of motivating media mentions. Who wasn't interested in staying youthful and healthy?

Greg Parker, the clinic's marketing director, was calm and confident that the evening would go perfectly. It was his premier, and everything had been planned, rehearsed, double and triple checked. Even with so much riding on this one evening, he seemed exceptionally self assured. Dr. Shepherd, the medical director, was as nervous as a new father, but not nearly as nervous as Jeff McGonagle, the CEO. Sawyer Wiles, chief financial officer, was taking deep breaths while eying the bar. This event was costing the company plenty, and he'd apparently be fine once he had a drink. They'd invested a fortune in developing the clinic, and the financial future was about to begin.

Alice Winters, the plastic surgeon, and Diane, the clinic's nutritionist, were both obviously excited to be part of this extravagant affair which was beyond anything either of them had ever attended. Connor Nelson, the physologist, was rehearsing what he'd planned to say to guests regarding the importance of individualized physical activity programs, even though he'd been instructed to simply socialize.

Eva Blackwell, molecular biologist and lab director, looked fantastic in her shimmery gray sheath. Her sophisticated, short, dark hair drew all eyes right to her dramatic face. She radiated elegance and dignity. This was indeed one no-nonsense woman. Perfectly proportioned although only five feet four, she had the demeanor of a woman of stature. Eva wore a necklace tastefully accented with small diamonds and large black pearls, a carat of diamonds in each ear, and no other jewelry. Not even a watch to detract from her face and necklace which pointed to the cleavage revealed by the deep décolletage of her simple, elegant dress.

After brief introductions to the major players, Stuart left Melody and Marisa on their own. They toured the clinic with other guests, amazed at the scope of the facility. Stuart was busy mingling, networking, and accepting congratulations from his client for a job well done.

Melody and Marisa had spent days shopping for something perfect to wear for this occasion. Melody had been looking forward to the event and knew Marisa was dreading it. It was Marisa's first social event without Grant and Melody understood it would be difficult at best. Marisa had inherited Grant's half of the agency and even though she wasn't an active partner she did have a responsibility to be present.

As extra incentive Melody reminded Marisa she'd finally get to lay her eyes on Eva, who Melody had assured her was a very real and very important client.

"Yes Marisa, there is an Eva, and she's not only a client, she's a big client. Let's go talk to her."

"You go. I think I'll go out on the patio and get something to eat, and then I think I'll go home. This is much too difficult. I know Grant worked hard on this account, and now..." Marisa swallowed hard and attempted to smile. "I didn't want to offend anyone by not coming, but I think a few more minutes and I will have fulfilled my duty."

"You do whatever's comfortable. Leave me here alone with all these smiling strangers," Melody teased. "I don't know a soul here beside you and Stuart, and he's way too busy schmoozing to pay attention to me. I'd go home with you, but I spent too much on this dress not to wear it another few hours. Anyway, I do want to find out more about this place and what they do. I still think all this anti-aging stuff's a lot of sizzle with little substance. And don't you dare ever tell Stuart I said that."

Marisa's conspiratorial smile vanished as quickly as it appeared. "This is way too uncomfortable for me."

"I know. I'm so sorry." Melody's voice changed from compassionate to questioning. "Marisa, I have to ask this. I don't know exactly how to put this. I've been wondering. Well, do you ever think that maybe something or someone caused Grant's heart attack? That it wasn't just a heart attack due to natural causes?"

Marisa's eyes became moist and sad. She shook her head no.

"No, Melody. I think he just died young. You can't cause somebody to have a heart attack. I think it was just, unfortunately, a bad heart no one noticed until it was too late. He would have liked this party." Marisa hugged Melody, turned, and bolted for the front door.

Melody was left heavy-hearted by Marisa's sadness and distress. She still felt there was something perverse about Grant's dying although there was nothing concrete to make her suspicious. There was no evidence that should make her have these persistent, niggling thoughts. So why, she wondered, did she feel deep down that something was amiss? Maybe her questioning was her way of coping with her friend's untimely death.

Melody hoped meeting some of the doctors and administrators at the clinic would take her mind off Grant. She walked over to Eva and the group of fashionably dressed strangers talking together. Stuart had briefly introduced Melody and Marisa to Eva when they first arrived and Melody thought she would be interesting to talk to. The group laughed at something, then the conversation stopped dead as Melody approached. Melody suddenly felt snubbed although she tried to convince herself it was just coincidence and bad timing.

"Hello, Melody," Eva drawled in a dignified, overly gracious tone. "It's such a pleasure to meet you. We've been so happy with Stuart's involvement here at the clinic. He's quite brilliant. But I'm sure you know that." Eva didn't make any effort to introduce Melody to the rest of her companions.

Melody forced herself to smile. Suddenly she would have given a year of her life to say something rude to Eva, but she knew how much the clinic account meant to Stuart. Still, she didn't like the way Eva's overtones seemed to imply intimacy with Stuart. Melody instantly disliked this stunning, obviously successful, remarkably brilliant, icicle woman without knowing anything more about her than her voice and appearance.

"I was so sorry about Grant's passing. He'd been working closely with us in the beginning. What a wonderful man. And so young. I miss his dynamic energy and wonderful sense of humor. He certainly had a way of charming us here." Eva spoke in an endearingly tender tone paced so slowly you could interject whole paragraphs between each of her words. The effect was spellbinding in a strangely intimate way.

Was Eva gushing over Grant? Or was Eva merely being sociable and Melody being a mistrusting bitch, overly sensitive to this beautiful woman's words and speech? There really wasn't any implication of anything just because of the way Eva spoke about Grant and Stuart but her voice managed to imply she knew both men better than Melody did.

"We all miss him. Especially Marisa. It's been really hard on Stuart, too," Melody added in perfunctory dismissal and immediately felt stupid for having said the obvious in her attempt to gain back the high ground of her relationship with both Stuart and Grant.

"I know. We talk about it." Eva seemed to be one who liked to push the parameters of deportment to the edge.

Melody couldn't wait to exit this tense little group but not without first injecting some clever rejoinder. Melody looked at the men and women around her who seemed to be used to Eva's behavior. They displayed no overt signs of discomfort by her arrogant tone even though the very air around them seemed slightly more electrified than before Eva spoke those few words to Melody.

"Funny, Grant never mentioned you. He spoke highly about everyone else here. Oh, wait, Stuart did mentioned some caustic, arrogant woman he had to work with occasionally. That must be you. So happy to have a chance to meet you. Lovely party, isn't it?" Melody remarked unfalteringly to the rest of the group. She smiled a belittling smirk at Eva. "Excuse me. I see an intriguing guest I've been wanting to talk to." She nodded to the group she hadn't been introduced to and she was off, relieved to be away from the hub of malevolent ions radiating from Eva, but worried sick about what her irascible outburst could do to Stuart's personal relationship with this major client. Her spontaneous parley could end up costing Stuart this whole account. Melody was astonished and horrified by her lack of control over her words even though she was well aware that verbal self-restraint was never one of her strengths.

Stuart will kill me, she thought to herself as she turned on her heel and walked purposefully away from the group.

Since there was no one else she knew at the party, she blindly headed as far across the room as she could manage, toward a complete stranger, and warmly said, "Hello, Ted. It's so good to see you here," as she extended her hand. "Oh, I'm sorry. You're not Ted. You looked just like him from across the room. Sorry," and feigning embarrassment she made her way outside straight to the bar.

Not-Ted, the stranger, followed her to the bar. "I hope you're not too disappointed. I'm Russ Daniels. Are you a doctor here at the clinic?"

"I'm a psychologist, but not here. Melody Fox. I have an office downtown. My husband owns the advertising agency that handles this account." She bit her lip unconsciously at the thought of the damage she'd likely done seconds before. "It's quite something," Melody remarked as she viewed the exterior of the building from the patio in the fading dusky light.

"I think this place will do quite well," Russ acknowledged. "Anti-aging is a growing field with the possibility of changing the whole pattern of diseases and disabilities associated with aging. The economic impact is staggering. The timing's just perfect for opening this clinic and Scottsdale couldn't be a better location. Boomers aren't thrilled with becoming old and incapacitated even though they spent most of their lives on too much self indulgence. Now they want to be magically made instantly healthy for the next fifty years. Don't you think that's a little nuts?"

"I haven't really thought much about it," Melody confessed, suddenly embarrassed by her lack of opinion.

"Ah, you're not forty yet, are you?"

"No. I'm not." This man was either very interesting, or nearly as insolent as Eva.

Melody couldn't distinguish which. "So, what brings you to

this party?" she asked, hopefully changing the subject to lighter small talk.

"I'm a reporter for CNN's HealthMatters. Your husband's done quite a job of promoting the Scottsdale Anti-Aging Clinic. We'll be broadcasting a small feature on it and I'll bet you a drink we won't be exclusive. So, who's Ted? Is he here? What are you drinking?" Russ asked without missing a beat.

"Margarita, please. Rocks and salt. There is no Ted," she confessed only slightly embarrassed. "Just had to get away from an annoying person I was tangled in conversation with. Actually, it wasn't a conversation. I was listening to her being haughty and I replied with a bit of overzealous venom I'm afraid."

"And what made you pick me?" Russ asked his question as an attempt to draw from Melody that she was attracted to him.

"You were the farthest person away from the woman I was talking to."

Russ laughed a deep, rumbling, all encompassing laugh that made Melody smile then grin, then laugh, which made Russ laugh louder, which then made Melody laugh harder.

"Who was it you were talking with?" Russ managed while he gulped for air between peals of laughter.

"I wouldn't dare divulge that to a reporter." The comment started them laughing again, much more laughter than the remark called for. They were caught up in something that had nothing to do with their words.

"Come on, I'll never tell," Russ burst into explosive laughter.

"Right. A reporter who keeps his mouth shut," Melody managed through another fit of chortles.

"That's not even funny," Russ sputtered trying to keep a straight face.

Melody's side started hurting. "This doesn't look good in front of the bar. Let's just quietly move over to that wall." They were still struck by the laughing jag when Melody caught Stuart's disapproving glance. Unfortunately, the sight of him talking with Eva of all people, plus Stuart's irksome look, as though she were a misbehaving child, started her off again. She nervously considered that he might already have been told about her comments to Eva and awful consequences were soon to follow, but still Melody couldn't control her outbursts of snickers. Finally, Melody and Russ composed themselves and sighed repeatedly regaining their breaths.

They were absolutely silent for about three minutes, when intermittent guffaws were launched again. Trying her best to compose herself, Melody thought it best to change partners.

"Well, Not-Ted, this has been fun, but I'd better mingle. Nice meeting you." He was definitely not insolent. He was opinionated, maybe cheeky, but not rude or insulting.

"And you, Melody. Here's my card. Call me any time you need a laugh." They smiled into each other's eyes, shook hands and Melody knew they could be very good friends or maybe more. No, that was simply a fantasy of the moment.

Stuart considered the evening to be a success. The grand opening was receiving exactly the reception he'd hoped for. The executives of the Scottsdale Anti-Aging Clinic seemed to be very pleased except for Eva who seemed to be miffed but remained silent. She remained aloof, slightly brooding, and preoccupied when they all gathered to go over the success of the evening.

"Now, that was a grand opening!" sighed Dr. Clark Shepherd who had never seen a medical facility open with such panache.

"I think that separated us from any other clinic that might try to compete with us," smiled Greg Parker.

"I think it went well." The understatement was Jeff McGonagle's contribution to their self-satisfied round of comments.

"I'll drink to that," added Sawyer Wiles as he picked up a half bottle of champagne and went around refilling everyone's glass.

"Congratulations, Stuart," Eva finally spoke, nodding at him while gloating in overt self importance. Eva's slow speech with overtones of sexuality often contrasted markedly with the actual words she spoke. It added immensely to her mystique. Eva was a captivating enigma. One would hardly expect a woman who spent more time in the company of lab rats than people to be so beguiling in a social setting, or a business situation for that matter. Everyone but Stuart seemed oblivious to her undercurrent of overtures. "Clark got some local coverage and I think he'll get some national exposure, too."

Clark nodded his thanks to Stuart and lifted his glass. "I expect we'll be scheduling patients first thing tomorrow."

"I was interviewed by CNN and NBC news and I'm sure they'll both broadcast part of the interview," Eva continued as though Clark's comment was never spoken.

Stuart worried that Eva was mocking his PR efforts, but he was beginning to think it was more of a strange, flirtatious cerebral toying with him. Throughout the evening she had stimulated him mentally and aroused him physically, although Stuart would never do anything to jeopardize his relationship with Melody. This verbal jesting with Eva was harmless fun, adding just a a bit of excitement to his regularly scheduled work.

He was pretty sure of that.

6

Melody's outbursts amused Stuart. In fact, it was one of the characteristics that endeared Melody to him when they'd first met, but never in their history together had her words held the possibility of such an important financial implosion for Stuart and Melody's economic well being.

"How could you, Melody! You realize you jeopardized the whole agency talking to Eva like that! Shit. When Eva told me what you'd said to her I was appalled. You could have ruined me—us—the whole staff at work!" Stuart's frustration raged while he paced back and forth, unconsciously driven by explosive energy.

"I said I'm sorry a million times."

"But you're not."

"No, you're right. I'm not sorry I said what I said. She was rude, offensive, malicious. She hinted at gross improprieties about Grant's character—and yours—and I got so reviled by her damn insolence I just blew. I knew she was goading me. I couldn't help it. She made me so red-hot mad I couldn't think. Words came out before I had a chance to stop myself. I'm truly sorry if what I said hurt the agency, but I'm not sorry for what I said." Melody slumped down in a chair, disgust changing rapidly to concern as reality set it. "Do you think you might lose the account? Have they said..."

"No, it's all fixed. I took care of it. Eva isn't pleased with you, but she admits she's caustic and arrogant and she doesn't think those are necessarily negative attributes. I'm just thankful you didn't say anything worse." A rudimentary flicker of pride from somewhere way back in the far reaches of Stuart's ego began to brighten his facial expression, softening the glare of his eyes, slightly raising the corners of his lips into a hint of an oncoming smile he could no longer contain. "When she told me about what you said to her, my first reaction was to strangle you, but then I felt this kind of primal, guttural thrill—a real rush—that you would do that. You would verbally brawl over me!" Stuart put his arm around Melody's waist, taking her other hand and twirling her around in a small, tight circle then dipped her backwards in a swift, romantic move, lowered his baritone voice and boomed roguishly, " You love me, don't you, darling. You can't help yourself. You're madly, uncontrollably in love with me."

"Yes, madly, insanely in love with you. More than that, I'm relieved you're taking the whole episode so well," she laughed, "but, regrettably, I've got to go to work right now, so let me go. How 'bout we pick this up tonight and see where it leads us...." Melody whispered affectionately.

Melody didn't have any break in her patient schedule all day—booked solid until six pm. It was still hot when she finally headed out to check on Janice Makowsky, her pro bono client who had just been committed to County Hospital by the Phoenix police. The drive from Melody's Scottsdale office to the hospital took nearly thirty five minutes with construction slowdowns that never seemed to end. She cranked up the air conditioner to full blast and directed all the vents to blow full force directly on her face and hands. She slipped an old Harry Connick, Jr. CD into the CD player and was comfortably cruising along the freeway headed west when suddenly her usually controlled, desperate need for changes in her life erupted like an electrical current that buzzed in her ears, crawled on her skin, and rose in her throat. Every day at work was now a rerun of the previous day's discontent.

"Keep doing what you're doing, you'll keep getting what you're getting." The insipid platitude popped up out of nowhere. The familiar refrain on the Harry Connick CD could have been composed specifically for those taunting words. "Keep doing what you're doing, you'll keep getting what you're getting," she sang louder and louder, bopping with the beat, keeping time tapping her ring finger on the steering wheel. Melody was so consumed by the moment she drove right past her exit. When the song ended she grasped the impact of what had been subconsciously decided over the past five miles. "I can't go on doing this. Yes, I need a change, and this is the time. Right now. Not someday. When the time is right, the decision is easy." Melody had given that exact advise to patients and friends countless times. Now she heard her advice directed at herself.

Melody drove into the hospital's physicians' parking lot forcing thoughts of Janice Makowsky to take center stage in her mind. All ideas of changing careers would have to wait until after this patient.

"I'm Dr. Fox," she spoke to the receptionist in the stark hall. "I'm looking for my patient, Janice Makowsky. She was brought in this morning."

The volunteer at the desk gave her a circumspect look then checked a computer screen and pointed toward the elevator. "Third floor, north."

Janice had been brought in by the police for causing a disturbance in front of a supermarket. She'd been swearing to customers that she was Hillary Clinton looking for her son of a bitch husband. As Melody continued reading the police report, she saw that Janice had grabbed a customer who was exiting the supermarket and scared the shopper half to death.

"Janice? I'm Dr. Fox. Remember me?" Melody asked in a kindly gentle voice. "You came to my office and we talked. Remember?"

Janice nodded, but her vacant, terrified eyes said something completely different. Janice had no memory of Melody.

"Please," Janice begged, grabbing the edge of Melody's sleeve, "make them stop screaming at me. Stop it! Stop it! Stop screaming at me!" she yelled releasing Melody and covering her ears with her hands.

Auditory hallucinations. Typical of unmedicated schizophrenia. Often the voices schizophrenics heard commanded them to do appalling things, drowning out all of their own thoughts. No wonder patients screamed back.

"We'll try to get the voices to stop. You missed your medication, Janice. What happened to make you leave the group home? Do you remember?"

"They're trying to poison me," she whispered conspiratorially to Melody. "You've got to save me. Get me out of there. Can you do that? I can't eat their food or I'll die. The medicine is poison, too. I'm safer on the street eating out of garbage cans. At least I won't be poisoned." In profound desperation, Janice grabbed both of Melody's arms, extreme fear and panic evident in Janice's face. "They want to kill me. Don't send me back there," Janice pleaded with a formidable terror apparent in her constricted pupils, rapid breathing, and frantic screeching.

"I won't make you go back until you feel okay." Melody hated lying. She hoped Janice could stay in the hospital until she was better.

Then Janice screamed in a voice loud enough to be heard outside over the noise of traffic in the street. "Don't send me back there! They'll kill me!"

"Okay. Okay. We'll take care of you here." Melody's voice and smile could have calmed a grizzly bear, but not necessarily a schizophrenic woman battling her derisive demons.

Melody continued her session with Janice for an hour and then wrote up her assessment to add to Janice's file. Dr. Otero, the hospital psychiatrist, would be in to check her and her medication within a half hour.

Melody knew her patient was fortunate to be admitted and given a bed. More often than not, all beds in psychiatric hospitals were full. Whenever a new patient was brought in, someone else was released whether they were capable of caring for themselves in the outside world or not. The best case scenario was when a patient could be sent home to a caring family and continue outpatient counseling, but most often these hapless patients had lost touch with their families after series of painfully failed attempts of dealing with screaming and countless episodes of running away. Melody was painfully aware of the fact that most schizophrenics need much more care than a family can give.

Often schizophrenics function quite well in a supervised group home, but unfortunately patients are sometimes released prematurely to fend for themselves in a world they don't trust and can't understand. Eventually they'll be picked up off the street again for disturbing the peace or some other infraction of the law, and brought back to a hospital but only until someone new needs their bed. They'll be released when someone new needs to be admitted. This outrageous cycle has been going on since the 1960's when lawmakers concluded mental institutions were horrible, degrading places that failed to provide mentally ill patients with an adequate level of care—and that was very often true.

Somewhere in the collective genius of the U.S. Congress, a resolution was dictated by non-scientists and non-doctors to put an end to ineffective treatment in mental hospitals by simply shutting them down. Mentally ill patients were expected to get themselves to community mental health outpatient centers and clinics for superior care. Their plan never worked—and never changed. Nearly half of all homeless people are mentally ill and could likely be off the street, functioning in society if given proper medication and supervision.

The neighborhoods of the homeless mentally ill unfortunately lack facilities for the care they so desperately need, Melody brooded. Huge numbers of unmedicated, confused, and mentally tortured individuals are left to their own resources which are often at a childish level, or worse, a constantly tormented disorientation. The incompetent system infuriated Melody so profoundly that she scarcely made sense whenever she discussed the issue.

As she was leaving County Hospital she paused at the admissions desk, a growing shadow of uneasiness engulfed her from the inside out. But she couldn't say a word. Her mouth opened repeatedly, like a salt water grouper, but nothing came out.

"Yeah?" asked the same disagreeable receptionist she'd encountered when she'd first entered the hospital.

"Do you have an Eileen Lewis here?" Melody finally asked assuming a veil of authority to cover her anxiety and apprehension asking a question with such staggering ramifications. Melody had no idea what she would do if the answer was yes.

"Patient or employee?"

"Patient." Melody's voice was nearly inaudible as the word 'patient' seeped through her dry, nervous lips. "Patient," she repeated more resolutely.

The admissions receptionist checked her computer, repeated the name, and asked Melody how to spell it.

"No, we don't have no Eileen Lewis here. Was she supposed to be admitted today?" The receptionist asked as if it were a normal inquiry.

"No. I don't know. I thought maybe she was here. Thanks."

An illusion of Eileen as Melody remembered her appeared—a sixteen year old tall, slight, girl dressed in strange clothes. Her dark, limp hair ended bluntly just below her ears. She'd be around forty five now. When Melody was a newborn, her sister Eileen was a normal ten year old. Melody only vaguely remembered her sister ever living at home. Eileen had been in and out of hospitals from the time Melody was six. By the time Melody was in high school, Eileen was already in an assisted living facility. She came home twice, each time a painfully emotional disaster for Melody and Eileen's parents. That much Melody could remember distinctly. Eileen would be difficult and disruptive at best, incessantly accusing their mother of attempting to poison her. She would refuse to eat and screamed at the dinner table. She often locked herself in her room for days at a time which included more screaming episodes and some strange conversations with people who weren't there.

Eileen was diagnosed as schizophrenic in 1971. It was a devastating diagnosis to Rose and Gerald Lewis, Melody and Eileen's parents, yet, in a way it was a relief to know, finally, what was wrong with Eileen. Eileen's doctor prescribed anti-psychotic medication, but Eileen was convinced the medicine was the means to make the voices' demands come true, and death would surely be the rapid end result of taking her medication. She did everything in her power not to take it and was very inventive. When she could be coerced into taking her medication, which was not often, her behavior became more normal. When medicated, Eileen would be coherent. In those more lucid, medicated moments, Eileen described herself as "feeling like I'm treading mud. Slow, thick, and muddled."

Eileen had run away from the assisted living facility in 1974 and ended up living on the street somewhere for nearly a year. She was found by police who arrested her for vagrancy. Fortunately, Eileen was hospitalized instead of jailed. She was medicated again during that hospital treatment, and finally recalled her parents' phone number and address. Melody vividly remembered her parents getting a baby sitter for her, saying they were going to bring her sister home. Melody had misunderstood and was excited by the thought they'd be bringing home a new baby sister. A sister she could play with and take for walks in the stroller. Not the frightening, screaming sister she barely knew and didn't really like. Her parents brought Eileen home with high hopes regardless of the dismal outlook reported by Eileen's doctors. There was only about a thirty percent chance that Eileen would ever be a healthy, self sufficient adult.

Rose and Gerald's hopes and dreams for Eileen's recovery were quickly dashed. Even with her medication and treatment, it became clear immediately that Eileen could no longer function outside an institution. Not even the depths of unconditional parental love managed to push away Eileen's demons. She ran away again, and had not been heard from since.

So, today on this late summer evening in the hallway of County Hospital in Phoenix, Arizona, two thousand miles from Pleasant Valley, Iowa, where she had last seen her sister years ago, Melody thought of Eileen when she looked at Janice Makowsky in the hospital room. Melody's promise to see that Janice got sufficient care and attention went beyond the professional boundaries Melody tried so hard to maintain.

Melody rushed out into the fresh air trying not to look like a woman who had just committed some unspeakable atrocity. She ran to her car and took off into the unhurried traffic, changed CD's to Claude Boling, turned up the volume to just below piercing in an attempt to drown out all thoughts of Eileen, and drove toward home without noticing the shadows of early evening that customarily brought her a sense of calm.

Without realizing where she was going, Melody had driven from the hospital right into the midst of Phoenix where homeless faces lined McMannus Street looking for their doorway for shelter for the night. Stark, vacant eyes watched her car slowly proceeding down the street of lost souls. People whose lives had been strangely forfeited by default of their own brain cells' failed wiring lined the streets like fragments of litter left by a throw away society.

"What am I doing here?" Painfully she acknowledged her subconscious had sent her looking for her sister again. "I wouldn't know Eileen if I saw her. I could drive right by her and I'd never know. Anyway, she certainly isn't in Phoenix. Looking for Eileen here is like looking for lost car keys under a street light when you know you lost them on a dark corner somewhere. This is senseless." Yet, as she continued slowly down the ghastly godforsaken street she was still thinking of Eileen. "Let her go," Melody willed herself. "I'll never find her." Melody felt a discordant connection to these street people and a deepening ache to do something constructive for them for Eileen.

It was pitch dark when she drove into the garage, secure in a loving home with all the pleasantries Stuart and Melody had accumulated over their five year marriage. Nothing like Janice or Eileen would ever know. Melody tried to ease her sadness by convincing herself that schizophrenics don't realize what they don't have. All she could do was help those she could treat. Even one person's life is never insignificant.

Stuart was moody and quiet when Melody walked in. It was strange behavior for Stuart who was naturally upbeat and positive.

Neither Melody nor Stuart spoke at first, both in need of comfort from the other and sensing, as couples do, that neither one had it in them to give. Melody's heart was first to melt like a Popsicle left out on a metal lawn chair on an Arizona summer afternoon. She loved Stuart dearly, and seeing him so dejected made her heart heavy. It wasn't what their morning conversation lead her to expect as a homecoming greeting.

"Hey. What's wrong? You look like you lost your dog. What is it?" she gasped. "Did the Anti-Aging Clinic...."

"Fisher and Fox lost another account today. The Burgermeister account this time. That's two in a row. This is a major financial loss, Melody." He sat motionless except for his swirling of a glass half full of something colorless on the rocks in his left hand.

"But you've still got the Anti-Aging Clinic, right?" She was staggeringly worried and feeling guilty.

"Yeah, but that makes the clinic our biggest client now, and it's not good having a new account be that financially important. That one account is over eighty five percent of our total business now. That's a dangerous ratio. One wrong move, we lose that account—there's no more Fisher and Fox. Want a drink?"

"Yeah, I think so. What about a contract?"

"A contract is about as binding as a sticky note if they decide they don't like your work or whatever reason they choose to make up. They could sabotage my work a thousand ways and make it look like my fault. Or, they can make a change in management and I could be out. On a whim. Without any real reason. You can't work with someone who doesn't want to work with you, contract or not. I hate this." His anger began to compete with his overriding gloom.

"Well, you'll get a couple new accounts." Melody tried to be upbeat as she poured herself a glass of wine. Attrition is part of the business. You've told me that over and over again. You win some, you lose some, right? Or you lose some, you'll win some." She tried with everything she had to restore Stuart's normal self confidence.

"The trouble is now I'm so busy with the clinic I don't have time to go after new business." Stuart was silent, then he breathed quietly as if to keep his thought from becoming a self fulfilling prophecy. "I don't know if I can do this without Grant." Until now he'd been able to keep that monstrously frightening thought at bay, kept it from reaching his lips as if that would keep tragedy from happening. Stuart ran his hand through his hair as he always did when he was troubled. He exhaled a long audible sigh and took another gulp of his drink. "And Grant's irreplaceable. How could he go and die on me?" Stuart looked up at her pleading for an answer he could grasp, his eyes a cold smoky gray green, as dark as a low, threatening storm cloud.

Melody went over and sat on the arm of the overstuffed chair and cradled his head in her arms, holding him close to her, feeling tension, anger and grief pour from his heart singed with a flicker of fear from a burning ember deep down in his soul. She slid into Stuart's lap.

Melody took a slow, steadying breath before asking the question that had been bothering her ever since Grant's funeral. "Do you ever wonder if maybe Grant didn't die of a heart attack? Do you ever think maybe there was something that caused Grant's death?"

"Honey, you were there in the emergency waiting room with us. The doctor said it was a massive heart attack."

"Yeah, but what caused it?" Melody moved away from Stuart and sat in the corner of the couch.

"A bad heart. Fuck. He had a heart attack. He died," Stuart exploded, his emotions mixing, melding, and erupting. He took a long swig of his drink and immediately became quiet. He looked away from Melody before continuing. "No. I don't think it was anything but a heart attack. It happens. Every single day I wish he were still here. I can't do the work of two of us and I can't ever replace Grant. The work to keep our agency viable is killing me. I'm trying to hold on. I don't want to lose it, but truthfully, I'm worried, Melody," he whispered.

He got up and went over to the bar and poured himself another drink. "It seems as if anything and everything's gone wrong over the past few months — Grant's death, losing two clients, the damn stock market — everything seems to be conspiring to keep me from enjoying what's left of my life."

Melody instinctively remained quiet knowing nothing would ease his morose mood. She'd just let him wallow for a while and be a good listener. Instead of his predictable response, Stuart mirrored her silence. They simply sat together for a long time.

Emotional stress always made Melody hungry. Tonight she was starving and finally got up to fix something to eat. Surprising Melody yet again by his sudden change in temperament, Stuart grabbed her on her way to the kitchen, held her close and tightly in his arms. She hardly recognized the emotionally volatile Stuart Fox she faced that evening.

"Come into the kitchen with me. Let's get something to eat." Rummaging through the refrigerator she found some cheese and opened a box of crackers.

"Did you ever go through Grant's office?" How could she have let that slip out? She knew when Stuart had had enough but she was more curious than cautious.

"Marisa wanted to do it alone. I don't know why, but she asked me not to. It was excruciatingly, painfully sad to watch her, and yet I couldn't help myself. I couldn't not watch. She took some pictures he'd had on his desk, it looked like a few papers out of a drawer—a coat he'd left hanging on a hook, and that's about it. She sat in his chair for a long time—oh, his coffee cup. She held his moldy coffee cup and sat in his chair for a long time. Just sat there. Finally I couldn't take it any more and walked away from the doorway. I still hadn't gone in myself and after Marisa's visit I decided I had to."

"Was there anything—anything at all that would give you reason to believe he didn't just have a heart attack?" Melody couldn't fathom why she was continuing this conversation, but now couldn't stop herself.

"Leave it alone, Melody! He had a heart attack. I went through his appointment calendar, feeling like a lousy thief or sadist or I guess a combination of the two."

"And?"

Stuart shrugged wordlessly.

They nibbled on cheese and crackers in silence.

"Have you ever wondered if anyone wanted Grant dead?" Melody questioned Stuart between crackers.

"Drop it!"

Stuart looked across the counter into Melody's pained and troubled face. "I'm sorry." His heart swelled with deep love for the woman he'd just yelled at who normally made him feel lucky to be alive. "I don't know how I'd survive if it had been you. I'd be so lost without you, Melody. I love you more than life itself."

"And I love you more," Melody answered. "Except when you get ornery."

"Let's go away. A long weekend somewhere. Can you get away this Thursday? We can be back by Sunday. I need time with you. Alone. I've got to get away from work."

"I thought you're so busy—"

"I am. I'm so far behind I can't even find the beginning of what needs to be done yesterday, but I can always make time to be with you. I need you with me for a few peaceful days away from work."

7

"Puerto Villarta? You mean Mexico?" Melody questioned, unable to hide the surprise and disappointment in her voice. "No, no, no...Santa Fe," she responded, holding up navy and brown fleece moose robes she'd just bought, smiling a beguiling, suggestive grin. "Mountains, snow, cool nights, cozy fires, moose robes—" Her voice, sexy and enticing, contrasted sharply with the practical bulky robe she was waving like a matador.

Stuart smiled, then grinned, then laughed. Melody loved making Stuart laugh. It seemed to her his quintessential laugh escaped from some deep and hot, lusty place inside him. That she could cause him to laugh so readily and so easily was what had first caused her to want to spend the rest of her life with him. No one had ever responded to her sense of humor the way he did.

Stuart and Melody were as opposite as two people could be, balancing the ying and yang of each other's lives and delighting in their differences. To take off for the beach or mountains was just another one of many opposite ends of the spectrum where Stuart and Melody often found each other. They were used to their dissimilarities and the more distinctly different, the more challenging it was to convince the other, and the more fun they had trying. They were both aware that Melody caved in more often than Stuart and generally enjoyed the consequences.

"Oh gosh," Melody whispered in a flirtatious, breathy voice. "Maybe a secluded cabin in the woods, no people but us, solitude, quiet, fresh, cool mountain air—" She batted her eyelashes, trying to tempt Stuart, knowing he wasn't easily tempted.

"Glorious white sand, shimmering endless ocean, rubbing suntan lotion on each other, Latin dancing—" He put one of his hands on his stomach and one hand in the air, his hips swaying as he danced the mambo, then grabbed Melody's hand and swept her close to him, grinding their bodies to the salsa rhythm he invented on the spot, spinning her around under his arm, then winding her close to his body, still holding her hand, twirling her away from him, ending in a dramatic dip and a sweet, lingering kiss.

Puerto Vallarta was looking better and better.

"I'll exchange the robes. Come with me first." She took his hand and led him to their bedroom. Stuart very willingly followed, coupled behind her, swaying to his continued whistling salsa.

"Oh my god, this is breathtaking!" Melody gasped as the cab delivered them to their resort on the beach. They checked in and raced to their room to get the most out of four hedonistic days of vacation. Melody put on her new swim suit and cover up, put some oils and lotions into a bag, picked up her sun glasses and book and was ready to go. Stuart changed, grabbed the CD player and some CDs, a couple towels, room key, money, and they were off.

"How's this?" Stuart asked, ready to stake claim to what would become their territory on the beach for the duration of their vacation.

"Absolutely perfect."

There were few people in this particular area of the beach which was exactly what Melody had longed for. The sky was cloudless cerulean blue. The sun cast shimmering diamonds on the soft waves of tranquil, transparent blue green ocean. The white sand was as fine as powdered sugar, without a trace of seaweed. The quiet was interrupted only by the soft repetitive murmur of small waves rolling eternally onto the beach and retreating into the ocean again.

"Drinks, sir?" a voice interrupted their reverie.

"Sure. Two Margaritas. On the rocks, no salt." Stuart looked at Melody for confirmation.

"Mmmmm. Perfect, except I want salt," murmured Melody, already on her back stretched out on her blanket, eyes shut, absorbing the sunshine, the heat, and the ambiance of paradise.

"How 'bout some suntan lotion before you fry, Melody. I don't want you burned and untouchable after we finally managed these few precious days together."

Melody smiled, sat up, and took the offered bottle of lotion, squeezing it onto her arms and spreading it over her skin then repeating the process on her legs, on her chest, and neck. "Will you do my back?"

The day was resplendent for both Melody and Stuart in its simplicity. "I haven't felt like this since the last day of school before summer vacation when I was about eight—completely stressless! No watch to watch, no appointment calendar, no patients, no reports. Ahhh, this is sheer heaven.

"No deadlines, no phone calls, no clients, no agenda."

Not quite true for Melody—she did have an agenda. Tonight she hoped they'd start the family she longed for.

They shared an intimate dinner in what had once been a small house now turned into a cozy restaurant of five small rooms with ceiling fans slowly revolving the warm air that blew softly through gauzy curtains. Candlelight was the only light, bathing everything in a soft golden glow. A guitar was played by a musician singing unknown words undeniably expressing love and desire.

"Three more blissful days with my beloved wife," Stuart began, lifting his wine glass in a toast. "I love you more than all the stars in the sky, the sand on the beach, and the fish in the ocean."

"And I love you, too," Melody whispered. Tonight, back in their room after this romantic evening would be the right time, yes! And timing, Melody believed, was as important as breathing.

The evening had been sublime but some instinct warned Melody to put off the mention of children, inexplicably feeling it would ruin the bubble of perfection. Maybe it would be better discussed at breakfast. Not in their hotel room. They still had three nights left. That night they made love tenderly, gently, increasingly ardent, impassioned, fiery, until sated and drained they lay tangled in each other's arms, the breeze from the open window blowing over their sweat drenched bodies. They peacefully listened to each other's breathing and kept time with the rhythm of their hearts until sweet sleep overtook them both.

Morning began with a distant church bell pealing the hour, punctuating the soft sound of lapping ocean waves, inviting all who could hear to slow down and match the repetitive relaxing cadence of eternity.

On the way to breakfast Stuart picked up a stack of rack cards of things to do in Puerto Vallarta since it was hard for Stuart to hang out on the beach doing nothing for long and he'd reached that plateau the previous day.

"I'll have an egg white omelet, dry toast, orange juice, and coffee," Stuart ordered from the petite Mexican waitress.

"French toast, throw his egg yolks in my French toast, extra syrup, fresh fruit, and coffee, please." Melody smiled at the young girl taking their order. "What's with the omelet? When did you become concerned with egg yolks? Did you have a bad encounter with a flock of chickens lately?"

Stuart smiled his lazy, sexy smile. "No, but the Anti-Aging Clinic guys explained some aging stuff to me for their brochure and it just makes sense to me to at least give up egg yolks. Some of the things we eat actually shorten our lives. I'm forty two. I want to live a long, healthy life. I'm just gonna do a few things that might help me live longer. You never know when your time's up. I want a lot more of these sunrises with you. What've I got? Maybe twenty five more healthy years? Maybe? Maybe less."

Melody wasn't surprised by Stuart's depressing attitude toward aging. She'd heard it before. She tried to make light of his concerns and change the direction this conversation was headed. Stuart had given her the perfect lead. Now was the time—

"We could have grown kids and grandchildren by then."

"Melody, not again. Not now. Not during this, our first escape together in—how long has it been?"

Although disappointed in Stuart's response, Melody wasn't willing to give up. "I don't know how long it's been. Stuart, we said we wanted a family. There's nothing new about the idea. Why not now?" She tilted her head and smiled, taking his hand in hers.

"Come on, Melody," he laughed, sounding patient and only slightly uncomfortable, but an undeniably abrupt, underlying testiness brought an end to any further conversation for the rest of their breakfast.

"Damn," Stuart said, angry at himself. Then in a more gentle tone he added, "Let's go, Melody. I can't sit here any longer. Take a walk down the beach with me. Let's not let the next three days be ruined by anything." He signed the breakfast bill and beamed hopefully at Melody.

"Agreed," she responded trying to ignore her lingering disappointment.

They walked barefoot in the surf leaving footprints that were erased with each succeeding white foamed wave, then they headed down the beach, past a few sunbather's lolling peacefully in the sun, past motor ski rentals, hobycat rentals, deep sea fishing charters, parasailing captains, scuba and snorkel rentals, and locals selling straw hats, bags, and typical tourist trinkets.

"This vacation's just made me realize how much I want to live, you know, not just exist from day to day. Not just go to work and come home and go to work again." Stuart was focusing on each step he took, not looking at Melody.

She waited silently for more, sensing this might be a prologue to something about to be changing her world as she knew it. Melody's protective hackles rose. She didn't like the feeling she was getting from the electricity between them.

"I want to experience more. I want to play more. I want to feel more. I don't want to die without having lived. I never told you about the dream I had about Grant and me." Stuart related the dream he remembered so vividly, being old, infirm, and left behind. "Life's just too damn short to be so measured — so full of demands and restraints. And responsibilities. Someday is already here and nearly gone for me. Maybe not for you. Maybe you can't understand what I'm going through. The realization that my life is more than half over is worse than awful. I don't want my life to end. I want to fill up every minute with whatever I want to do. I need to feel alive." He'd been walking backward, facing Melody, then stopped and turned to face the ocean, arms spread wide to encompass the universe and was silent for a small eternity. "Do you understand what I'm saying? Something's missing."

"Of course." Then after a weighty pause Melody continued, "No, not really. I don't understand at all. I thought we had a perfectly wonderful life. I thought you thought so too. What's missing?" She nearly added 'other than kids which would give you reason for living' but for once in her life kept her mouth in check. Instead she stood firmly in the shallow water, feeling the waves wash over her feet, the sand crumbling away beneath her footing, waiting for an explanation she didn't want to hear.

"I can't bare to lose a single minute of the rest of my life. Let's do things we've never done. Let's just be spontaneous. Let's go parasailing. Let's go scuba diving." He turned to Melody, putting his hands on her shoulders, turning her toward him — connecting them. "Let's devour this place, not lie on the beach, or sit in restaurants. Let's go off and explore. That's all. Don't be worried," he continued, sensing her reticence, seeing trepidation rise in her eyes. "This isn't something bad. This'll be invigorating — good for both of us."

He's having a mid-life crisis and it'll be good for both of us, Melody thought. This had come out of the blue as far as she was concerned. Hit by a Mack truck, she followed her husband back toward the tourist section of the beach and listened to him get two parasailing tickets.

"Welcome aboard," the captain grinned. "You're gonna love this," he said as he piled his passengers into his dinghy, cranked the engine, and headed toward a handsome thirty five foot motorboat farther out in deep water.

Melody had never been a thrill seeker, and hoped she'd either have the strength to resist the persuasive goading of her husband, the captain, and the others on the boat, or that if she'd give in she'd still survive. She didn't even like water with fish in it. But it was a beautiful day, and it would at least be a lovely ride out on the ocean, so how bad could it be?

"Do you serve drinks on this boat?" she asked.

"We've got a little courage in a bottle for those who need it," the captain laughed.

Hap, the instructor on board explained what to do. "The wind takes you right up and you control your ride by maneuvering the straps from the parachute to the seat. The closer to your body you hold them, the father down you'll go since less wind will catch in the umbrella of the parachute. If you want to go up, you spread your arms out and that'll catch more wind and lift you up. Simple. The boat'll run in three wide circles and then bring you back to land on the dock right over there. Who's ready?"

Stuart went to the front of the group, volunteering to go first. Melody headed to the little bar on board as her knees began to knock. She began to shiver just watching Stuart put the harness on. "Dear Neptune," she begged, "get us through this alive."

"I'll have a rum punch, easy on the punch."

She heard Stuart shout with unbridled delight as he was lifted into the air. She couldn't help but beam at his uncontrollable joy. You could hear him yelping and hollering, whistling and hooting, and having the time of his life. Maybe he was on to something with this new quest to live every moment of life. "I'll go next," Melody heard from very near-by. "Oh, shit," she blurted realizing the words had come from her very own lips. She downed her drink as the boat swung around for the third time, depositing Stuart on the dock. He was still whooping like a cowboy. "Shit," Melody repeated.

"Ready?" Hap asked as he checked Melody's hooks and lines. She swallowed hard, closed her eyes, and nodded yes. Up and up and up the wind caught and carried her. It was scary as hell, but glorious at the same time. Her heart was pounding and her hands were sweating so much she was afraid they'd slip off the grips. The wind hollered in her ears and her hair trailed behind her until the boat took a turn and her hair blew in her face obliterating her view. She managed to fling her hair back with a toss of her head, and she could see she was higher than the palm trees at the back of the beach. "Fantastic. Whoohh!" she whooped. "Incredible!"

When it was time to get down she completely forgot everything she was supposed to do. Hap and Stuart were yelling instructions at her but she couldn't hear. The boat slowed down and she landed in the ocean, sea water gushing up her nose. She came up coughing and sputtering, but shining as if she had single handedly caused a minor miracle.

"Oh Stuart, that was glorious! Incredible! Undeniably the most astonishing experience I've ever had."

Stuart was thrilled that Melody had enjoyed their first step in sharing a more audacious, adventurous rest of their lives.

After an exhilarating day filled with sailing, parasailing, and more exploring along the beach they sat at the bar under a thatched roof, sipping powerful yellow rum drinks and listening to a Mariachi band. They watched the sun dip into the ocean, hoping to catch the illustrious green flash appear at the final fraction of a second the sun disappeared.

"Let's never go back to Scottsdale," Melody muttered, dreamily. Between the thrill of parasailing, the heat of the sun, and the icy drink, Melody was nearly ready to fall off her stool. "Let's live here in this hut and go parasailing every day. We could get our own boat and take people out for rides." She was only slightly drunk, but completely intoxicated from the euphoria of the day. Maybe it was the other way around—slightly euphoric and completely drunk. "We can send the bar tender to Scottsdale, and we'll stay here in his hut."

Stuart laughed his masculine, seductive laugh, and kissed his wife sweetly on her sugary rum lips. "Mmm. Come on, my love," he said as he signed the bill. Melody began stroking Stuart's thigh. "Not in the hut," he whispered in her ear. "Let's go to our room—"

She responded with a goofy smile that embarrassed Stuart at it's undeniable suggestion although no one was at the bar to see her except the bar tender who was used to sexual innuendoes. He nodded knowingly with a grin so wide you could count all his teeth.

They were both just past slightly burned from being in the sun too long. "Let's take a shower, then let me put this lotion on your sunburn. It's going to hurt tomorrow," Stuart chuckled as he held his drooping, relaxed wife.

"Shower, yes. Touch my sunburn, no. Touch anything else, definitely."

Although they'd been married five years, Stuart had never seen Melody this drunk. He laughed, anticipating a wonderfully erotic evening if she didn't fall asleep first.

The next thing Melody knew it was morning.

"Tomorrow's the end of this glorious escape. I don't want to spoil our last day—but I can't put this off any longer, either." Melody took a slow, deep breath of courage, knowing full well she shouldn't pursue this right now.

"Stuart, let's start our family now. This is as perfect a time as it's ever going to be. We can afford a family. You'll only be sixty when our son or daughter graduates high school. That's not old. You want to live every minute of your life? Well, damn it, life is about kids and being a family. You'll be a wonderful father. I'm sure of it," she cooed hesitatingly. Anxiety, apprehension, cold fear, and a hang over were beginning to interfere with her resolve to continue.

They were sitting outside on the hotel restaurant's patio, having just ordered breakfast. The brilliant bougainvillea flowing gracefully over the wall behind contrasted with the darkness that intensified in Stuart's smoky green eyes.

"Melody, we've discussed this before. Before we were married we agreed we both wanted kids, and we also agreed to wait." Melody nodded in understanding, full of hope, yet made uneasy by the dark, serious expression on Stuart's face and the tone of his voice. "Melody, I love you, but..."

Oh, god—no, she thought, not 'I love you but....'

"I don't want kids now. I don't mean just 'now.' I did want kids, or at least, I tried to want kids. I didn't lie to you. But I don't now. I don't want us to have any kids."

Melody's heart stopped beating and nearly shattered into a thousand pieces hearing those unbelievable, unexpected, unbearable words.

"I don't want to share you, Melody. Not your time, not your

body, not your heart. It's selfish, I know. Maybe it's stupid or even childish, but it just shows how inept I'd be as a father. It's the truth." He leaned forward to be as close to Melody as he could, reaching for her hands, for a physical connection to the woman he so dearly loved. "I don't want to change our lives. Having a kid would completely alter what we have. I want us to be free to be spontaneous. To take off and go places — like this trip and other trips. I want to experience the world and do things with you. Together. Just us."

Melody tilted her head back as if she could deflect Stuart's outlandish unexpected words and make them skip into outer space where they would be taken away forever. She shockingly realized in that instant that Stuart had been subtly trying to tell her this for a long time. Part of her knew it, her consciousness never accepting it. She had a sudden, overwhelming feeling of having been swindled out of everything she'd ever wanted. On the heels of dismay grew a flicker of anger. She was nearly dizzy from her emotions swirling in chaotic turmoil.

"You can't mean this. You can't just change your mind." Sputtering, Melody continued. "We agreed we wanted kids. I want us to be a family. I want to have your children," she spoke softly, lovingly, trying to cajole Stuart into changing his mind. "There's plenty of me to go around." She forced a laugh, a hint of a hesitant smile breaking through her pained expression. "If we don't have children, who do you expect is going to take care of us when we get old and feeble?" Her attempt at softening the severity of their differences had no impact on Stuart's expression.

Stuart put Melody's two hands together in his and began unconsciously stroking them with his thumbs. "I don't want to be a father, darling. I don't want to play catch and go to school programs. I don't want a mess of toy trucks all over and noisy little neighborhood kids invading our house."

"How 'bout dolls and dainty, quiet, feminine tea parties? We might just have girls, you know," determined to mine any prospective vein of possibilities.

"Melody, I've thought about this for a long time. I didn't want to say anything to you until I was sure. I am sure now. I definitely don't want kids. I just want you."

"You'll still have me, plus a couple of living, breathing little people—a part of us who'll love us and need us and bring us joy and happiness and fulfillment. Don't you see that?"

"And interrupt us, and exhaust us, and whine, and cry, and get sick and need care."

"Sure. That too. But that's not all. I can't believe you're saying these things. It's absurd. You're not that selfish." Oh god, she wished she hadn't said that.

"I'm selfish because I don't want to bring up a kid when I know I'd be a bad father? Come on, Melody. Let's end this for now. The best I can do is say that right now, I don't want kids and that we'll talk again sometime, okay? That's as far as I can go. I'm open to talk about it again but not now—not today and not tomorrow. It's all the time we have left before we go back home and back to our chaotic schedules in the real world."

Seeing no alternative, and even considering his okay a small ray of hope, Melody agreed, at least out loud.

She silently nodded in agreement. They were both quiet for what seemed like hours, picking at the remnants of their breakfast, sipping cold coffee, and avoiding each other's eyes. For Melody, the vacation was over.

What if he doesn't change his mind, she thought with alarm. She considered getting pregnant 'accidentally' but that would be a lie that was beyond her ability to live with. She didn't want an unwanted child to come between them. She needed Stuart to want a child as much as she did.

The rest of the morning was tense with both of them thinking their own separate thoughts. Finally Stuart broke the silence that was strangling their last full vacation day. Impulsively Stuart suggested they try scuba diving lessons.

"I just don't want to do anything right now but hang out here and get over this—this unexpected, unbelievable change of heart of yours."

Stuart's face twitched slightly at Melody's words. "Well, I can't just sit here. I think I'll take some lessons and go diving this afternoon. I don't want to make you go, but it's something I really want to do. Okay? I'll make it up to you." Stuart kissed Melody here, there, and everywhere.

"All right. All right. Go play with the fish." Relieved to have the formidable silence between them breached she smiled at Stuart's promise, her anger and dismay slightly dissolving. "Just be in one piece when you get back. I'm going to stay here. Maybe take a walk, or a bike ride, or maybe I'll rent some snorkel gear and hang out with the fish, too."

"Do you give snorkel instructions?" Melody asked the guy at the water sports equipment shack on the beach. This vacation was not going well. "I've never snorkeled. It's not hard, is it?"

The suntanned, muscled masculine beach maven behind the counter appeared to enjoy the way she hesitatingly asked about snorkeling, as if wanting to try it and at the same time wanting a good reason not to attempt it. The shirtless, barefoot blond dive shop clerk hopped over the counter and gave Melody an encouraging smile.

"There's nothing to it. I'm Chip, and I can show you how in a five minute lesson. Here's a mask, snorkel, and fins." He picked them out and showed her how to fit the snorkel through the strap and tighten it. "Now put it on and breathe through your mouth. It's important that your mask is tight or you'll get water in it, and you're likely to try to breathe through your nose. If you do, salt water will be sucked right up into your sinuses. It's good if you're stuffed up, otherwise it's not so good. Let's go down to the water and give it a try." Chip grabbed his own snorkel gear and hung up a "Back Soon" sign. They headed toward the water's edge, putting on their fins in the softly lapping surf.

They walked out into the ocean about thirty feet, the peaceful water still only up to Melody's waist. Chip put on his mask and Melody mimicked his exact motions. "Put the mouthpiece in your mouth and bite on it. Now breathe through your mouth." Melody tried breathing through her mouth, but she was also breathing through her nose as Chip could tell by the contraction of the nose clamps.

"No, just your mouth," he laughed. "Hold your nose closed with your hand over the nose part of the mask if you have to. Now, breathe through your mouth, and once you've got it, let go of your hand on your nose. You really don't need that. Sometimes though, it helps get people started. Put your face in the water and try it.

Surprisingly, it worked, although Melody was breathing so fast she would have blacked out if Chip hadn't motioned to her to pick up her head. "Not so fast. Breathe normal. You have to breathe slower or you'll hyperventilate. Try it again."

Melody tried again, making an effort to breathe slowly.

"Perfect. That's just right." He beamed at Melody like he had just taught her the secret of the universe. Now, next lesson. If you get water in your mask, tip it back and blow air out of your nose. If you don't clear it, you'll likely inhale that salt water I told you about."

Melody practiced clearing her mask a few times. It was much harder than learning the breathing.

"Okay. Now. Lesson three. This is important. Clearing your tube. If you don't keep your head on the very top of the water, or if a wave comes by and rolls over the air intake of your tube, you'll get water in your tube instead of air. Not a problem, just don't inhale it. You gather up air from your lungs without breathing in, and with a strong exhale, you blow the water out. Like this." He put his head in the water, lowered it below the water level and Melody watched as a flume of water not unlike that of a small whale, streamed upward.

"Try it."

Melody put her mouthpiece in her mouth and carefully rested her head on the top of the water. She lowered her head to try what looked so easy, and inhaled salt water.

She picked up her head, took out the mouthpiece and coughed, sputtered and choked.

"You don't quite have it, yet. Blow out, don't suck in."

"Geez," she wheezed and coughed some more. "I'm not trying that again. I'll just stick close by and be careful not to get too deep.

"It'd be better if you knew how to clear your tube, but you'll be okay if you stay where you can stand up. There are some schools of fish just over there," he directed Melody to a spot down the beach where a few floating sunburned backs and black tubes could be seen sticking out of the surface of the water. "Bring the equipment back when you're done and you can charge the equipment to your room. The lesson was my treat. Just don't get in over your head if you can't clear your tube."

"Trust me. I won't be going farther than I can walk."

Snorkeling was a surprisingly exhilarating experience although breathing underwater continued to be a strange phenomenon. Swimming with the brilliantly colored fish was incredible, or maybe it was the experience of again, doing something she'd never done before that was providing the thrill. Either way, it was a much welcomed switch from the disturbing news from Stuart earlier in the day.

After floating around for a while Melody became comfortable, her breathing measured and relaxed. She was engrossed in the new world she was playing in but when she saw a sting ray swim near her, she'd had enough, grateful to be able to say she swam with a sting ray, but even more grateful when he turned around and headed out to sea.

She ran into Stuart at the dive shop returning his scuba gear as she turned in her mask and fins. "Buy me a drink?" she asked flirtatiously, as if he was a stranger and she was trying to pick him up.

He didn't catch the innuendo. Stuart was so exuberant after his dive, he could hardly contain himself, bubbling over with superlatives, none of which seemed to equal his out of control elation.

"That was phenomenal. Fabulous! That was the most fantastic experience!" He slicked back his wet, curling hair with his hand. "Next time you've gotta try it. You should have seen the fish. And the wreck. We went through this old wreck with fish swimming all through it. What are you doing at the dive shop?" he finally asked, realizing he had expected to find Melody lolling on the beach.

"I'm returning my snorkeling equipment. I saw incredibly colorful fish and even a sting ray," Melody excitedly shared her experience with Stuart, but he didn't hear her, still racing in his own adrenaline high. Chip heard, though, and he winked at her, a knowing wink that acknowledged her thrill.

"Can't go for the drink. I'm working, but thanks anyway," he teased, knowing she'd meant it for Stuart and seeing that he hadn't heard her.

Melody smiled a gracious, slightly flirtatious thanks, and she and Stuart headed back to their room. The magic of their four day escape was over. The echo of a rift in the foundation of Melody's life took away all the joy of her tropical paradise no matter how hard she tried to make the best of their last night.

One phrase continued to haunt Melody through her troubled sleep: No children for me. Not ever with Stuart.

Melody was quiet on their flight back to Phoenix. She pretended to sleep the whole way, but was hardly relaxed. She was contemplating the rest of her life never being a mom. No children for me. She felt an abysmal sadness at the thought.

"Flight attendants, prepare for landing." And the vacation they had looked forward to with such pleasant anticipation was over.

8

"Either something has to change quickly and drastically or I'll lose my mind!" Melody blathered to Marisa in utter frustration while sitting in Melody's office sharing a quick lunch of sandwiches Marisa brought in from Max's Sandwich Bistro.

"I sure wouldn't feel open to blabbing my worst perversities and lurid fantasies in here," Marisa joked, looking around Melody's small, drab, utilitarian office.

"But, that's exactly what I'm after—personal histories of depravity, perversity, and bizarre sexual experiences. That's what makes this profession so rewarding for us voyeurs." Melody let out a long audible sigh and pursed her lips. "In reality, there's nothing rewarding about this whole career anymore. I'm close to giving it all up. Just burned out. I've been brooding and agonizing about changing careers for a while now—doing something else—maybe I'll be a Ph.D. truck driver or snorkel instructor. No, I can't be a snorkel instructor, I haven't conquered clearing my tube underwater.

"The old nagging need for change that I've tried so hard to ignore has mushroomed into a craving for something more. More, I don't know what. Something more engaging. Something I can sink my soul into. I do nothing but work, you know? My private life is somewhere between minuscule and nonexistent, and I'd say that's a conservative understatement."

"You just got back from Mexico! Did that trip have anything to do with this change of heart?"

"I don't think so." Again Melody was lying, and this time to her best friend. "Maybe. Stuart's always had a tendency to be possessive but I didn't mind. At first I found his craving for all my attention alluring. After five years of marriage it's not quite so romantic. It's closer to stifling. Am I whining?"

"Just on the verge," Marisa answered.

"Ya know, different friends are important for different reasons. Some you turn to for moral support, some you call on for their opinion, knowing they'll give you confirmation of your own ideas, and those you need to give you a jump start with a kick in the rear. Some to listen to you cry, and some to make you laugh. You have to fill all of those for me, and I'm grateful beyond belief for your friendship." Melody watched Marisa smile and ball up the remnants of her lunch. Melody needed to tell Marisa about the news Stuart sprang on her in Mexico before she disintegrated in a wash of profound sadness.

"Melody, Molly McGinnis is here. Should I send her in?" Gail interrupted, knowing full well Marisa was still there.

"Sometimes I wish I could grab Gail by her vocal cords and cram the meaning of the word tact down her throat."

"I'd better get going anyway." Marisa got up and threw away her garbage while heading for the door. "I have to run errands then pick the boys up from school. Lunch was fun."

What I wouldn't give to be in a rush to pick up a couple kids, Melody contemplated. She shook off her self pity leaving invisible remnants of it all over the room.

"Thanks so much for lunch. That was a great surprise. I really appreciate it. Let's do this more often." Melody realized at that instant how poignant it was that Marisa, the one who was widowed just a few months ago seemed less lost than she herself, the happily married, somewhat successful career woman.

Melody walked Marisa to the door and said goodbye, took a quick breath to transform back to self confident Melody Fox, psychologist. Professional listener.

Finally, blessedly, another work day came to an end. Melody picked up the mail in her box on the way out the door. On top of her journals, newsletters, magazines, and bills was a brochure that caught her eye. It advertised a two day symposium on schizophrenia being presented in Atlanta at the Southeast Psychology Association's Regional Conference. Normally Melody would have pitched the piece unless it had some design element she thought Stuart might want to see. There were conferences and seminars closer to home, but now with two clients, Molly and Janice both dealing with schizophrenia, and her recurrent thoughts of Eileen, the brochure aroused her interest at least enough to take it home and look into it. Any other day Melody probably wouldn't have looked at the brochure. Timing, that perpetual trickster, had played itself right into Melody's hand.

In the car on the way home her thoughts wandered to the possibilities in Atlanta. Maybe Stuart could meet me there and we can spend some time together. A chance to talk again without work intervening between us. A chance to revisit the subject of children.

There were many times lately Melody wanted to scream. It seemed Stuart had degenerated from the successful, exuberant, sexy ad executive she'd always known, into a nagging shadow of the confident man he'd been. And he was often a petulant, bad tempered, cranky husband whenever he wasn't off on some quest for a new physical thrill.

I think I'll ask Marisa to come along instead. Atlanta with Marisa was a much better idea than going with Stuart. Maybe I'll fix Marisa up with Not-Ted, the guy at the clinic opening from CNN, whatever his name was. He lives in Atlanta. I still have his card. Just thinking of Russ or Ross, whatever his name was, engendered a smile that spread and grew into a chuckle then a hearty laugh.

Melody turned into Albertson's parking lot, went straight to the deli and picked up a rotisseried chicken along with fresh corn, strawberries, blueberries, and a half gallon of premium caramel chocolate chip ice cream—heavy on the cream. The strawberries and blueberries were to pacify Stuart who insisted on having some 'brain food' and plenty of anti-oxidants with every meal now. "His stress is doing more physical damage to his body than ten tons of blueberries can ever undo, I guarantee," she said out loud to an elderly stranger in the produce aisle, unable to withhold her acidic sentiments. She grabbed a bottle of wine at the display opposite the check out counter, paid her bill, and was back in her car in less time than you could say 'world famous Scottsdale clinic prescribes blueberries for eternal youth.'

Melody was barely capable of concealing her resentment of Stuart's recently acquired ornery attitude that often greeted her when she got home after he did, but she walked into an empty house which was quiet and calm. Melody tried to sympathize with the enormous stress Stuart was under running the agency alone—responsible for the incomes of the entire staff and all. She understood the agency was still dangerously off balance with the Anti-Aging Clinic being dangerously crucial in the financial mix of clients, but new business was sure to come his way.

Melody ate her chicken alone, reading the Southeast Psychological Association Regional Conference brochure and the Atlanta Schizophrenia Symposium again. It was in a month which gave her just enough time to clear her calendar, hopefully find a cheap airline ticket, and go for it. She needed the continuing education credits anyway and Atlanta would be a great escape.

With thoughts of the schizophrenia symposium on her mind, Melody impulsively grabbed her camera and got in the car as though possessed—blindly focused on her destination. She drove back into Phoenix, to McMannus Street—the street of homeless lost souls where she had driven by the congregants of hopelessness once before. The evening light was low, adding dramatic, long sorrowful shadows to the edges of the dismal, dreary atmosphere and surroundings. "I have no right to invade the lives of these lonely, hapless people," she said to herself, but she couldn't stop.

She felt a compelling, totally irrational need to capture the despair that everyone else ignored. Nothing in the universe was more important than capturing this minute, these images, and exposing these exigencies that were invisible to everyone else. Her heart beat rapidly, throbbing in her ears. She knew she didn't belong here, but at the same time she was the one person who did belong right here right now with her camera, recording a fleeting moment in lives that didn't have fleeting moments, but rather long, extended, unconnected sequences of bewilderment.

She pulled up to the curb on the driver's side of the one way street, and shifted the car into park, aware of only two things—taking pictures and knowing she shouldn't be here. Soundlessly, a scrawny man with long white hair and a scraggly white beard walked right up to her car door. There was a deep vacancy in his cornflower blue eyes which looked right through her, focused about three feet past where she sat. There was something Merlynesque about his presence. Magical. Mystical. Mad. He looked like an old man, but was probably fifty. He smelled particularly foul, yet there was a kindness that percolated through his outer layers of grime. He didn't say a word. He wasn't begging, he was just curious. Childlike. Not many people stopped in this neighborhood. She felt exploitative and purposeful and the same time.

"Hi. I'm Sue and I just want to take your picture," Melody stuttered in a soft voice, no idea why she used a fake name—he'd never remember her anyway. Slowly, she moved one hand from the steering wheel to the seat where her Pentax was lying next to her. She didn't know how he'd react. He might be as timid as a gazelle or as bold as a tiger. She just didn't want to do anything to cause her to find out. She wondered if his hands were strong enough to hurt her.

Melody hadn't expected to be taking close up shots. She didn't know what propelled her to come out here in the first place, but during the drive from upscale Scottsdale to downtown Phoenix, she had time to imagine documenting a moment of time in the lives of these street people through a series of quickly snapped photos. This particular man's face exhibited a road map of what once had been thoughts etched over remnants of what might have been. The crags of his face showed weather and wear but his blue eyes held a glimmer of a path to a mind inside. His image was too compelling to pass up. How fortunate that this particular person had walked up to her car with the last glimmer of daylight sinking low over her shoulder, highlighting those clear blue eyes. Melody hoped she would capture what she felt in his presence. "I just want to take your picture," she cooed soothingly as though she were talking to a troubled patient—or a space alien.

Her hands had begun to shake which was not good considering how close her subject was to her camera lens. She had a brief fraction of a second to decide whether to go slow and cajole this man, or snap a quick shot and scram.

Ever so slowly, while humming a lullaby she thought might soothe the stranger's soul, she picked up her camera, made some adjustments to the lens and shutter speed while she held it in her lap, steadying her hands before bringing the view finder up to her eye. He hadn't made a move. Melody wondered if he needed to breathe oxygen like the rest of us, or if he was already dead, and just his skin and bones remained visible on the street. You can't shoot pictures of ghosts, she recalled hearing, slightly amused. Well, if the photo comes out minus a person, I've seen a ghost all right. It seemed perfectly possible at that moment, looking at him so thin and pale, devoid of substance.

She snapped one extreme close up during which she held her breath and thought she might have captured the essence of a past, sane life reflected in his eyes — his current street life reflected in the rest of his face. Then she snapped another and another even though she could tell he was becoming slightly frightened and agitated.

"It's okay. Shhhh." She tried to soothe this hopefully harmless man whose space she'd just invaded, that piece of space likely being the only thing he possessed in the world. Mumbling incomprehensibly he turned and disappeared back into the darkened doorway he'd come from, arms flailing, back bent, head down.

Melody knew better than to get out of her car, yet her hand was already on the door knob, opening the driver's side door of her car. Her left foot hit something mushy in the gutter. She forced herself to quickly disregard all the possible things the mushy substance could be, and carefully balanced herself so she would get her footing on solid sidewalk. She left her car door open, engine running feeling better having a means of quick escape close at hand. "What the hell am I doing?" she wondered as her body kept going, walking toward a woman standing straight as a rod, singing in a scratchy voice without a tune — without a beginning or an end.

Melody took a quick look at her car, considering how easy it would be for someone else to get in and drive off, but still she slowly walked up to the singer wearing three dresses, a pale green one on top of a dingy one that may have been blue at one time, on top of something no longer distinguishable. She wore a pair of flip flops on her feet, and sang her heart out unto the heavens. Melody was no more than three feet away from the woman, and quickly snapped her camera three times with slight changes in zoom, focus, and exposure with each consecutive snap. The woman didn't even notice. She nodded, smiled, exposing a toothless grin, and continued singing. Melody took a few more photos, still feeling like a thief in the night. Stealing something from people with nothing.

She turned to take a quick glance at her car. Still there. Still untouched. She should leave now. She knew that if she had any sense she wouldn't be there in the first place, let alone out of her car, by herself, with total darkness not more than minutes away. She refocused her camera and took some long shots of people huddled in doorways. She zoomed in from where she stood and took some portrait shots. Another man, another woman, another rather indescribable person either man or woman young or old. Then Melody spotted a child.

She looked to be about five or less, Melody wasn't good at judging little kids' ages. Dirty. Sucking her thumb and holding on to the remnants of a pair of jeans worn by a tattooed, pinkish-blonde haired girl passed out on in a doorway. Melody froze. She couldn't move away. She couldn't move closer. While she tried to reason with herself that this child would one day be just fine, she knew she was lying. The little girl stared into Melody's eyes like a faun caught in a light. "It's okay. I won't hurt you. I just want to take your picture." But she wanted to do so much more for this little girl.

By now it was too dark to shoot without a flash, and a flash would destroy everything. Melody tried a couple long exposures first, then felt compelled to capture this little waif no matter what the consequences.

Flash! Shrieks and wails began from startled near-by crouched figures. Obscenities from the passed out mom. The woman singing began screeching "My Lord What A Morning" in a speed that was double what it had been a minute before and getting faster, louder, and higher every second.

Melody ran out of emotional energy, got in her car, closed the door, and roared off.

She could not shake the vision of the little girl holding her mom's dirty, torn jeans. She felt raw and brittle and as jagged as shattered glass fragments held together simply by will, not even paste. She was tortured by what she'd seen and felt staggeringly guilty for intruding into the lives of people too confused to know what was going on. Yet, in a conflicting vein, at the same time she felt validated by what she'd accomplished. These photos told stories of a world most people never saw nor wanted to acknowledge.

Stuart still wasn't home. She preferred some time alone anyway to digest what she'd just done. Stuart would admonish her like a child for having put herself in a potentially dangerous situation and she certainly didn't need that right now.

Melody was still dazed and not really ready to deal with conversation. She checked the kitchen table where notes were usually left. Nothing. Then she poured herself a drink, alone, which she'd never done in her life, and checked the answering machine. Two messages.

"Melody, it's me. Where are you? I'll try the office. I just wanted to let you know I'll be late. Don't wait dinner for me." Weird.

"Melody, it's me again. Where've you been? I tried the office about an hour ago. Anyway, as you can see, I'm still not home. I'm tied up with this project right now, and it's finally coming together so I don't want to stop. Don't call, okay? I don't want to be interrupted right now. I'm cookin'. Finally. Don't wait up. See you later. Where are you anyway?"

Melody felt Stuart get into their bed later that night, but was too deep asleep to see what time it was. Didn't matter anyway. She needed sleep more than a conversation with Stuart. Morning was most likely too close for comfort.

Stuart woke up late and came down to the kitchen for coffee just as Melody was about to leave for work. Melody had two shots left on her roll of film. Camera in hand, ready to drop it off to be processed, she finished the roll by shooting pictures of Stuart over his adamant protests, with his coffee cup in hand while trying to cover his face with his arms.

"I think I got good one. You look like a fugitive. Bye, honey. See you tonight." Melody gave him a half hug and a quick kiss as she opened the door to the garage to start her day.

Nothing had been said between the two of them about either Stuart's project nor Melody's escapade. They each went their separate ways which, Melody began to think, was becoming more and more the standard of their lives. She didn't like that thought at all, knew they should talk about it, then buried the thought.

As Melody drove past the Scottsdale Anti-Aging Clinic she growled and hissed at it. The clinic seemed to have devoured Stuart while becoming an enigma between them. "I just need more of a life! I'm not competing with an institution for god sakes. How can I get mad at the business that puts food on our table and keeps a roof over our heads?"

Her roll of film could only be entrusted to her favorite, professional film lab for processing. Melody was anxious to see if her photos came close to any of her expectations from her impulsive adventure the previous night. She visualized superimposing a homeless portrait over the morning shot of Stuart's protestations.

As soon as the photo lab opened the next day, Melody was there, waiting.

"These are good. You take 'em?" quizzed the older man behind the counter as if it couldn't have been her photography as he nodded toward the envelope she hadn't opened yet.

"Yeah. Thanks." She appreciated the compliment however backhanded it was. He saw photos from professional photographers every day so his opinion meant a lot to Melody.

Melody took the unopened envelope into her car and opened it carefully as if either a treasure or a monster might emerge.

They were good. Some of them, anyway. They showed anguish,

dispossession, and vacuity. Disorientation, childlike innocence, and — oh my gosh, the little girl. Fear and acceptance, ignorance and tolerance, years of futility already etched in the facial features of a five or six year old kid. "My god." Melody just sat there staring at her work. Her work.

It was going to be a long day at the office, made even more difficult to focus on her patients with those photos begging for her attention. "Either cancel the rest of this afternoon, or shape up Melody," she reproached herself. She checked her appointment schedule. Damn. Booked solid. Melody carefully laid the photos in her top desk drawer and noticed the hand scrawled note that she'd totally forgotten about. Melody tried to imagine who could have written the note and what could be 'NEXT'. No answers came to her immediately and she closed the drawer.

The Atlanta symposium brochure she had brought back to the office caught her attention. She simply stared at it for full two minutes.

"I'm going," and with that she filled out the application and faxed it.

After her last patient closed the office door behind her Melody sat back in her chair, studying her drab small dark office for nearly ten minutes. "I can't stand this office any more. No way. This is the perfect time," she vowed to herself and without another second wasted, she got up, walked out of her office to talk to Jamie Duncan or Pam Brock, the two partners in the practice.

"Do you have a minute?" Melody questioned as she knocked, then opened Jamie's door a crack, leaned forward and poked her head in.

"Sure, come in. Have a seat."

"I want to quit my job here. I'll give you two weeks if you want, but I'd like to quit right now."

"Just like that you want to quit? Don't you think you should give it a little more thought, Melody?" Jamie offered in a motherly tone with an accompanying nodding head that simply irritated Melody more. "Maybe a leave of absence is more what you need. We could accommodate—" She may have tried to convey concern, but her voice oozed with condescension, making Melody absolutely sure this was the right thing to do and the right time to do it.

"No, I want to quit. Now. I'll come back sometime tomorrow and clean out my desk if that's all right. Gail can reschedule everybody. No one's suicidal."

"You sure you want to do this, Melody? You're a good psychologist, you know."

Melody let a lengthy, uncomfortable silence fill the office before responding with a sharp edge to her voice. "You know, you've never said that to me before. I think it's too late now. And I'm better than good." Melody looked closely to see if Jamie's reaction was as dumbfounded as she hoped. Melody was certainly surprised by what she'd just said, but that was nothing new. She didn't realize the rancor that had been building inside her due to the total lack of support or encouragement from her bosses. "Life's too short to feel this way."

"And what way is that?" Jamie's voice sounded just like the wicked witch offering Snow White an apple.

Melody just smiled. "I'm outta here."

"What are you going to do?" Jamie continued.

"I have no idea...."

9

Melody picked up the phone after one ring as she sat at her kitchen table, unemployed for the first time in her post-graduate life.

"So, how's it feel to be unemployed?" It was Marisa.

"Mixed bag. It feels luxurious and it feels empty at the same time. I slept late, haven't showered or dressed, and all I have scheduled for today is to get to the office and clean out my stuff, return my key, and pick up a final check. I think it's going to take me all day to get going without my traditional beginning of the day to-do list. I can tell you one thing — it's glorious not hearing Gail's histrionic, noxious voice to start out my day."

"Well, I think you were smart to quit. You were definitely unhappy there. How'd Stuart react?"

"He was surprised to say the least, and kind of...angry...that I hadn't asked him for his opinion first. Geez. It's my life. It's not like my salary was that spectacular or even an important part of our total income."

"I have news, too. I'm employed! I'm now one of the hard working American taxpayers as of this coming Monday morning."

"Oh no, bad timing...I mean, congratulations, I really do. But I was looking forward to time we'd have to be women of leisure now that I'm not working. It's not my timing. It's your timing. Can't you wait a couple weeks or months? What are you sacrificing your freedom for? What about the boys?"

"I'll be working at the Three Sisters Gallery on Marshall Way. Just part time. They understand my responsibilities to my sons come first and that's fine with them. They have kids, too. I'm so excited! I'll be selling and eventually, hopefully, discovering new talent, putting together shows and exhibits and maybe doing some promotions. I hope, eventually, to be able to buy art for some of the corporations around here. That's the kind of job my degree in art history was supposed to get me. I've always loved that gallery and I think it'll be fun to work there. I just hope I don't spend all my income on art before I even get a check in my pocket. I know I could. Oh Melody, my own money! I'm so excited. I'm so jazzed, I can't sit here. Can I buy you lunch? Let's go now."

"You bet you can buy me lunch, but it's a bit early."

"Where do you want to go? How about Sammy's?"

"Sammy's," drawled Melody with an air of spurious refinement. Sammy's was a white tablecloth, fresh flower, business hangout not far from her office. Many big deals had first been launched among the movers and shakers of Scottsdale at Sammy's. "Okay. I'm warning you though, I'm hungry and planning on desert. I'll pick you up at eleven forty-five."

Melody considered bringing the envelope with her recent photos. She was nearly bursting with the need to share the results of her escapade. But this was Marisa's celebratory lunch. Another time would be better, more appropriate, but damn, she wanted to show someone now, and no one but Marisa would do.

At eleven thirty-five, Melody carefully stashed the envelope in her briefcase feeling as if she were carrying top secret microfilm.

She intended to leave the pictures in her car, but just in case the right moment came up, she wanted to be prepared.

Marisa and Melody waited with the crowd of dark suited executives, hungry lawyers and their hopeful clients. While they waited to be seated, Melody recognized Stuart's familiar voice carried over the hum of multiple conversations. She knew he hadn't seen her enter. Seated with him was a woman she recognized instantly—Eva Blackwell.

Melody involuntarily shivered as she experienced a vivid visual flash back of Eva at the grand opening and how much she disliked that woman. Her surprising discomfort seeing Eva and Stuart together rocked Melody. Why does this scene make me feel so alienated and ill at ease? There's nothing wrong with them having lunch together. Eva's a client. His biggest, most important client.

"Look. There's Stuart. With Eva." Marisa stretched out the three letter name with a pronounced, long 'E' that made her lips contort into a gruesome snarl. "Damn, she looks good."

"Maybe she's been playing with experimental anti-aging drugs," Melody snickered sarcastically, enjoying being catty.

"Melody. They can hear you!" Marisa whispered.

"No they can't. Stuart has selective hearing and he's listening to Eva. No, they couldn't have heard me." Melody shifted slightly so her back was to Stuart. "Don't let him see you, but is he looking this way?"

"I don't think so."

"Good." Melody decided to head over to their table. "Come with me and sneer at Eva."

"It would be a pleasure," Marisa smiled graciously as her privileged background had taught her, although it was pure insincerity.

Stuart was startled when he recognized the two women headed toward his table. He seemed more caught off guard than pleased and there was a fleeting, awkward silence in which Melody and Eva communicated volumes of unspoken dialogue.

"Melody? Marisa?" Stuart's voice put an abrupt end to the two women's silent communiqué. He brought his linen napkin to his face as if to wipe off his astonishment.

"You remember Eva." Practically tumbling over his words, he nodded from one to the other as he got up from his chair, scraping the legs against the floor, announcing to the whole room the awkwardness of the instant. Eva, it appeared, didn't know the meaning of the word awkward. She seemed to have three degrees of reaction. Cool, cold, and composed.

"Yes, sure. Hi." Melody said taking a breath.

"Hi, Eva." Marisa had much more self control. She actually included a warm smile with her greeting.

"What are you two girls doing here?" Stuart asked.

"Celebrating a business deal. And you?" Melody wanted to reply to Stuart's 'you girls' with 'you kids' but managed to control herself. The question was asked with as much chill as she dared knowing how important Eva was to her own financial well being.

Eva answered the question without giving Stuart the opportunity to answer his own wife. "We're discussing my latest research article that's about to be published and how we can get some extra PR out of it for the clinic," murmured Eva, smiling broadly, her words dripping with superiority.

"Um," Melody nodded as if publishing an article was no more important than daily flossing. Assuming an attitude nearly as cool as Eva's, trying not to appear impressed although she was, Melody was stuck for a finish to this terse social exchange.

Just then the Angel of Good Timing and Acceptable Exits appeared and sent the matre'd to announce their table was ready.

"Oh, our table's ready. Nice seeing you again," Melody managed. Stuart and Melody visually quizzed each other without uttering a sound. Melody leaned over and laid a sweet kiss on Stuart's lips before leaving.

"She is undoubtedly the most arctic female I've ever encountered," Melody whispered to Marisa when they were seated.

"You were pretty chilling yourself. What's the deal?"

"I told you what I said to her face at the clinic opening, didn't I? I shouldn't have said it, but it's the truth. Why can't I just ignore her and her audacious attitude?"

"I refuse to let her interrupt our celebration for another second."

"Okay. We'll just forget her," Melody emphasized with a flip of her wrist. "From what I understand she's only let out of the lab on rare occasions and spends most of her time coddling her favorite rats. Two of them actually froze while she was petting them, didn't you hear that?" They laughed too loud and diners' faces turned to look at them, some with reproach, some out of curiosity.

"So, tell me more about your new job."

The waiter interrupted, squarely placing menus big enough to hide a fugitive in front of each woman's face. He introduced himself as Richard, as if someone cared, announced the special of the day, and asked about their drink preferences, recommending a California Merlot while not moving a single facial muscle.

"I'll have a red Zinfandel," they replied in unison.

Marisa began a lively account of two of the three sisters she'd met so far who owned the gallery. "I can't wait 'till you meet them. They're witty and they're funny, and very perceptive. They definitely know the art world—and Scottsdale buyers."

For some reason Marisa's praise of the sisters aroused a flicker of jealousy completely out of context for Melody. Could Stuart's possessiveness be rubbing off on her? She didn't want any part of that, she swore to herself. Melody was feeling more than a faint flicker of jealousy about Stuart and Eva having lunch together, too. Nonsense. Stuart wouldn't think of an infidelity.

Listening to Marisa's eagerness, Melody became slightly dejected. When had she lost her exuberance for her own life and started replacing it with jealousy? She didn't know. Then Melody remembered that, yes, she did feel that wonderful exuberant unrestrained joy just the previous morning. It happened the moment she saw the photos she'd taken.

They ordered lunch and watched the tables around them wheel and deal. Melody overheard one man with a deep Southern accent talking to another man at the next table. His accent reminded Melody of the symposium in Atlanta.

"I suppose your new job puts a crimp on our trip to Atlanta," Melody sighed plaintively.

"What trip to Atlanta? When?"

"I got a brochure about a symposium in Atlanta. There's a lot of new research I'd like to hear about, and I need the continuing ed credits anyway...even though I don't have a job right now. I've never been to Atlanta so I thought it would be fun if we both went. You could explore Atlanta while I'm at the conference, or you could come down the last day and we could stay a while and play. I haven't been on a trip without Stuart since before we were married. I want you to go with me if you can. I think it would be great fun."

"I'm only working part time. It's possible I could take off. Oh geez, I haven't even started working and I'm considering asking for time off. What have I gotten myself into? What's the date? Maybe my parents could come stay with the boys. They'd love that. Oh, I hope it isn't during the PTA book sale. I promised I'd help with that. So, when is it?"

Melody grinned. Marisa was good for her. "It's next month. I sent in my registration yesterday before I could change my mind."

"Okay, get me the exact dates and stuff, and I'll work on it. Maybe I'll discover some not yet famous artists in Atlanta — make it a business trip!"

"All business already," Melody joked. "Marisa, I have something in the car I'd like to bring in and have you to look at — especially now that you're in the art world. No, wait a minute. Here come Stuart and Ice Lady."

Eva took a detour, and Stuart came over by himself.

"You're not Eva's favorite person on earth," Stuart stated with a bit of a bite to his words. "What are you doing here?" he repeated as if Melody had entered a restricted club she wasn't allowed in. Melody watched his thin lips quietly and slowly over-enunciating every syllable.

"I'm having lunch," Melody responded flippantly. "What are you doing here?"

"Hi, Stuart," Marisa said, although he hadn't even acknowledged her presence.

"Marisa just got a job. We're celebrating."

"Congratulations," Stuart responded flatly with only a brief glance in Marisa's direction, then he left to catch up with Eva.

The two women silently watched as he hurried down the hallway toward the front door and walked out with Eva. Melody felt like an abandoned left over.

"Now, what were you going to show me before Stuart interrupted us?"

Melody ran out to her car and and retrieved her briefcase. Wordlessly, she handed the envelope to Marisa. "I want your honest opinion. I want your critical eye to tell me the truth."

One by one Marisa took the pictures out of the envelope and studied each one intently and silently. Anticipation came close to driving Melody insane.

"That's good. Just look at them and don't say anything. I just had to share them with someone and Stuart would never understand. I knew you would."

"These are incredible photos Melody," Marisa finally responded.

"They're touching and gut wrenching at the same instant. They capture an instantaneous moment of a confusing life. They show horror and hope. Understanding of the misunderstood. These are wonderful. Especially these shots of the little girl." She then put all the pictures carefully back into the envelope and handed them to Melody. "What are you going to do with them?"

Melody shrugged her shoulders and took a long sip of wine. "These photos give me something, Marisa. A thrill. A reward. A satisfaction. They give me a little bit of that excitement you came in here with and I haven't felt that in a long, long time—until now. I want to show people what's going on carefully hidden away from the public eye and I want to show what I can do. I'm going back to take more pictures. Will you go with me?"

"Where'd you take these?"

"Just over in Phoenix on McMannus Street. Imagine what I can shoot in Atlanta—"

"Don't you go driving into homeless neighborhoods in Atlanta young lady! Is that why you want me to go with you? I wouldn't make a very good body guard, unless you consider that maybe I just wouldn't let you go anywhere even the slightest bit dangerous. You're damn lucky nothing happened to you in Phoenix."

"These people are harmless. They're helpless, homeless, and harmless. They need treatment more than anything."

"They need drugs and they've got guns or knives," admonished Marisa.

"Maybe some of them. Not the ones I ran across."

"These are wonderful, important photos. Maybe you can be my first artistic discovery for the gallery." Marisa arched her eyebrows excitedly.

"So, you really think you can go to Atlanta with me?" Melody asked.

"I'll start asking about a sitter, check the PTA book sale date, and see about time off. That sounds so strange. Time off. You be careful if you go out shooting more pictures, and no, thank you, I don't want to go to McManus street. I don't think you should go either."

"Two nights ago I felt compelled to grab my camera, get in the car, and drive. I don't even know what inspired me to do it or why I ended up where I did, but I'm glad I did. I'm revitalized. I want to take some daylight shots."

"What about dessert before going off to shoot hungry homeless people. It seems so decadent now, but Sammy's Tiramisu is the best I've ever had. Should we get two or split one?"

The office can wait 'till later, Melody impulsively decided as she closed the door of her red car and fastened her seat belt. Lunch had been too emotional. Between the high of Marisa's admiration of her photographic talent and her atypical uneasiness—jealousy?—running into Stewart and Eva she pitched all thoughts of packing up her office. She wanted a frivolous escape.

She drove to the Fashion Plaza on autopilot and parked near Nordstroms. Melody's mind was racing, picturing where her life would go from here. The conference in Atlanta. Yes, that was a definite. What she'd do with her professional life after that was questionable. She'd just stumbled upon a major life crossroad and felt ill prepared. Unemployed freedom was suddenly more unsettling than peaceful and laid back.

Melody decided to start at Williams Sonoma. I'll buy myself something I don't need and then make an elaborate desert with chocolate and pecans and cream in puff pastry or something.

Thirty five dollars and two bags of specialty food stuff plus a new lime juicer, a piping bag and tips, and a new wine bottle opener later, Melody was headed back to where she'd parked her car, still trying to concentrate on what she would make for dessert while trying not to be overwhelmed with thoughts of what she'd do with the rest of her life.

Melody had just learned the first lesson of unemployment: A day contains too many hours to ruminate about what might be in the near future. Or what wouldn't be in her future. Unexpectedly the conference in Atlanta had become the only scheduled event in her life. She'd focus on that.

She had to go back through Nordstroms to get her car so she decided to look for something to wear at the conference. She tried on three dresses and two pair of slacks, none of which fit her mood and new self image, and bought two pair of jeans plus three T shirts instead since her closet at home was full of suits and few play clothes.

She was only the tiniest bit worried about the rapid fluctuations in her emotional state of mind. It was normal to be a little on the fringe finding yourself abruptly facing major life changes. Quitting her job was definitely a life changing event, she reassured herself.

Melody got in her car and drove into Phoenix. She wanted to feel the contrast between upscale Scottsdale and downtown Phoenix again, just to add another jolt to a day full of antitheses. Besides, the only other thing she had to do was empty her office which was an unappealing idea at the moment and to make her gooey desert, which could wait.

She slowly drove through the same homeless neighborhood she'd driven through two nights before. As dismal as it looked at night with dark, eerie voids and creepy shadows, daytime was worse in some ways. The dereliction was more evident in the daylight. Decrepit doorways that some called home — gutters where refuse made it's last stop before decaying — a few lost souls wandering the sidewalk — no signs of flourishing life.

She took one last confirming look and was about to turn back toward her comfortable home in Scottsdale. Then, coming out of the doorway of a two story seedy old adobe building in the middle of the block she noticed a man of indeterminate age counting dollar bills. As he left, another man walked in the door. All Melody could see was a stairwell inside the building as the door closed. Was that ragtag assemblage a line of sorts — of people waiting their turn to go in the building and come out with money?

Melody was curious enough to get out and ask someone what was going on. As she opened the door and authoritatively got out, someone came up behind her and pulled on the strap of her shoulder bag.

Melody clamped her elbow tight to her handbag, pinning her purse close to her body, swatting and kicking madly at whoever was behind her still holding on to the strap of her bag. With a swift hundred and eighty degree turn the strap broke, releasing Melody from the thief's hold and she was face to face with her mugger.

"Leave me alone," Melody screamed into his face, kicking at his crotch but missing before she noticed he was the most pathetic, frail old man she'd ever seen. Maybe equal to the Merlyn-man she'd photographed. He was so thin and scrawny a big wind would have carried him away. He looked confused and forlorn and though she felt like a wuss, her furious indignation at being a victim immediately melted. "Don't ever do that again," Melody spat out as though she were the final authority here. Melody grabbed her purse with both hands, turned her body a quarter turn away from him, still staring at him furiously as she opened her wallet. She took out a twenty dollar bill and angrily stuffed it in his hand. "Get yourself something nutritious to eat."

His head tilted like a dog listening to a high pitch as she spoke, but he didn't respond.

"Can you tell me what's going on in that building over there?" she asked him quietly.

He just shrugged.

Instantly other residents of McMannus Street began to mob Melody, hands out pulling on her clothes, grabbing at her, begging for their cash as well. Melody knew she'd made a big mistake and quickly tore herself free. She ducked back into her car and took off not looking to see what fate might have befallen the thin old man. Hopefully he and the twenty dollar bill escaped safely together.

Melody brought her bags of absolutely unnecessary purchases into the house and set them down on the stone kitchen counter top. Instead of baking as she had intended to do, she went to her room and started going through her closet, pitching clothes and shoes she hadn't worn in years into a pile on the floor. Vehemently she purged her closet and then Stuart's, attempting to shed her reeling feelings of self indulgence, prosperity, and good fortune. She stuffed bag after bag with clothes, shoes, underwear, and then added a nearly new blanket for good measure.

On Saturday, still not used to being unemployed, Melody got up late and found a note Stuart had left on the kitchen table: Melody, I've gone skydiving. Love, Stuart. Yeah right, she laughed as she read the crazy note. He's probably at the office.

Melody punched Marisa's number on the phone. "I was thinking about taking a bike ride and wondered if you were home and wanted to go too?"

"Sure, yeah. It's another beautiful day and I'd rather do anything than wash the floor. Cleaning can wait. I'm probably not good for very long though. I haven't been on a bike in years. I'll have to see if my neighbor can watch the boys. Come on over."

They headed out leisurely on the gently curving, flat bike trail along Scottsdale's verdant green space. Riding two abreast, the conversation between the two thirty-something women of very different natures developed into the easy, friendly feminine confidentiality that they'd often shared before.

"I think I might get a dog." Marisa let out in a little giggle. "I think giving the boys something warm and fuzzy right now is a good idea. D'you ever consider getting one?"

"Are you kidding? Stuart wouldn't tolerate a dog. He doesn't even want kids." The words slipped out of her mouth. Although Melody had desperately needed to talk to Marisa about Stuart's revelation, she couldn't bring herself to say the words out loud to anyone until now.

"He doesn't want kids? What about you?" Marisa looked at Melody whose bike nearly wobbled off the path.

"More than anything in the world," Melody sighed. The connection between Stuart and Melody made its first small crack. The comfort of self deception was accidentally whisked away. There was no longer any way to deny the fact that a family of her own was what Melody most wanted in life. And Stuart did not share her desire.

No children for her. Not ever with Stuart.

The two friends rode in silence for a long while, Marisa being the kind of friend who knew when not to ask questions or make comments that wouldn't change anything.

When they returned to Marisa's house Melody stowed her bike in her Jeep Cherokee and gave Marisa a desperate hug. "Can I use your phone to call Stuart before I head back? He was already gone when I got up this morning."

Marisa nodded toward the phone and Melody called her home number first.

"Hello-o," Stuart sang in a wildly upbeat voice.

"Hi, it's me. You home? Did you go to the office?"

"Oh, Melody! Where are you? I've been trying to find you! I had the most glorious, unbelievable day and I couldn't wait to tell you! I went skydiving. Piggyback, of course. I jumped out of a plane! It was the single most enthralling thing I've ever done in my life! Remember parasailing in Mexico? This was even better! You've got to go with me next time."

"You really jumped out of a plane? I thought you were kidding this morning. I'm at Marisa's and about to head back home. See you in a few minutes." Melody was flabbergasted.

"He went skydiving! I think he's losing his mind!"

"I could hear him. He was practically screaming. Are you gonna do it?"

"I'm staying on the ground, thank you." Hesitantly, Melody confided in Marisa again. "Stuart's been different lately — almost like a different person. Ever since Grant died, Stuart's been consumed by needing more and more dangerous new experiences. Golf and tennis used to be too time consuming for him. Now he seems to be seeking physical risk. He's tried rock climbing, scuba diving, he talked about hang gliding, and now he's gone parachuting."

"He's a high risk kind of guy. Scuba diving and parachuting aren't all that unusual."

"Have you ever done either one?"

"No, but I'm not a high risk thrill seeker. What about you shooting pictures on McMannus Street alone at night? Maybe you and Stuart aren't as different as you think. Maybe it's Stuart's way of coping with loss, you know? What do they call it? Survivor's remorse?"

"Hey, who's the psychologist here? But you know, I think you may be right on target."

As soon as Melody stepped into the house from the garage Stuart grabbed her, hugged her in a swooping, swirling, circular motion, lifting her right off her feet.

"I did it, Melody! I jumped out of a plane."

"Why?"

"Because! Because I've never done it before. Because life's just too short not to fill it with everything possible." Stuart looked lovingly at Melody, and took her arms in his hands.

Yep, survivor's remorse, Melody thought to herself. "What's it like?" She asked, wanting to share in his excitement.

"You know what it's like to put your hand out a car window or out the sun roof when the car's going seventy-five miles an hour?" Melody nodded. "It's like that push against your whole body. And then you see the ground coming closer and then it's unbelievably scary, but once you slow down, it's not quite so scary. And then you land and it's amazing. It's such a thrill. Such a rush. I want you to try it."

Stuart's high scared Melody. She could almost hear another crack in a growing crevasse between them. What could possibly be next that she wasn't prepared for?

NEXT. She remembered the note she'd found in her office.

10

Just before noon on Sunday Melody slid her key into the lock at the psychology practice that had been her second home for three years and opened the door for the last time. She'd received a call from her ex-boss, Pam, that they'd appreciate it if she would please clear out her stuff as they had a replacement for her coming in on Monday.

"Dispensable. Disposable. That's how they always treated me," Melody ruminated as she walked into her familiar office carrying empty boxes to end this chapter of her life. She placed her psychology books in four boxes and then packed up her desk top things. Shortly she began emptying her drawers, opening the right hand top drawer first.

"The note...." Melody held the paper in her right hand, squinting, searching, digging in her memory to try to remember any time frame in which she had originally discovered the note. Whose handwriting was it anyway?

About to throw it away, she randomly flipped through her daily calendar which was the next piece of office paraphernalia to go in a box. She'd stuff it inside and keep it. As she flipped through the calendar, it opened to the Sunday Grant had died. That was about the time she had found the note. Memories of Grant's humor and ease flooded her. Melody smiled, filled with pleasant memories, immediately remembering Stuart the way he was before Grant died. Less cranky. Less reckless.

A sudden rumble of thunder startled Melody as there hadn't been a storm cloud in the sky when she had walked into her windowless office. The loud, low sound reminded her of the eerie storm during Grant's funeral. Weird, too, that she had just opened her calendar to the day he died.

"You trying to tell me something, Grant?" she asked as she slowly turned around in the office looking into corners and feeling spooked. "Am I right? Did someone cause your heart attack?" she asked the silence around her. "No one else thinks so," she said to the silence, looking from floor to ceiling and everywhere in between. "Stuart and Marisa both tell me it's my subconscious dealing with your dying. Who's the psychologist anyway?" she responded knowing there was a lot of truth to what they'd said.

Maybe it is time to give up the idea. Let it go. Let him rest.

"All right Grant. I quit."

Melody could hear lightening sizzle the heavens, followed by more thunder. Her skin prickled.

"I quit." she repeated, challenging the heavens to answer her. Silence. Nothing. She breathed a sigh of relief at the lack of response from Grant Fisher's ghost or Mother Nature.

"Next," she announced in two syllables as if she were an announcer at a carnival as she walked out into the reception room, boxes in her arms up to her chin. She mentally shrugged her shoulders since she still had no clue as to what the note was meant for.

The rain hadn't caught up with the thunder yet and it was still dry outside. Melody took one box at a time from the waiting room to her Jeep. Another crash of thunder caused Melody to look up. The sun was shining in spite of the thunder in downtown Scottsdale.

Melody then drove toward downtown Phoenix where it was now pouring as if the sky didn't care about the lives of those on McMannus Street. She sat in her car, camera in hand, waiting for the pelting rain to stop as it usually did within a short time during Arizona's summer monsoons. She looked out through her rhythmic repetitious windshield wipers that needed replacing. She focused on the doorway she's seen people coming out of and going into on her last visit. She was back now because she'd become obsessed with the need to find out if it was nothing or whether something was going on that authorities should be made aware of.

She couldn't see the doorway through the downpour from where she was parked. She could sit in her car and wait out the rain, Melody thought, or she could go out in the rain. Everything she had on was washable except her shoes — and her camera.

Waiting patiently was not one of Melody Fox's strong suits however. Out she went through puddles and pelting rain, heading straight for the suspicious doorway.

The street was quiet but the incessant rain was increasing and it suddenly became hail. Most hailstones were no bigger than peas, but big enough to hurt. Melody quickly headed toward the doorway and backed into the meager shelter the door jamb provided. Thunder suddenly crashed so loudly the building shook.

"Now what?" she asked herself. At least she knew better than to bring her purse with her.

She snapped a photo of the soggy filth around her, purposely taking a long exposure to blur the rainy reflections on the sidewalk. Just then she noticed a man standing in the rain — just standing there getting rained on without caring. Snap. Zoom. Snap. Snap again.

There wasn't anything else that caught her eye so she moved out of the doorway and turned around to take a picture of what had been her refuge. Snap. Snap. She backed up and took some long shots. Gray and dismal. Captivating effect through the rain. If only she could backlight the rain.

If she pulled her car up on the curb sideways with her headlights shining on the sidewalk and if she got on the far side of the car the rain would be lit between the car and the building entrance, she thought.

She walked back to her car and maneuvered into her seat, wet clothes refusing to slide over the leather. Her hair was dripping in her eyes as she looked in her rear view mirror and then in front of her before spinning around on the wet street, making a U turn and jumping the curb. She put the car in reverse and forward again, straightening so that the headlights would shine all the way down the sidewalk. She'd have to make this quick.

What photographers won't do, she admonished herself, realizing with joy it was the first time she'd referred to herself as anything but an amateur. She tried the title again. Photographer. Melody waited a minute before turning on the headlights and grabbing her camera. She got out of the car and focused. Snap. What luck! Someone was coming out the door. Snap. Zoom. Snap.

Suddenly she was hit from behind, her camera ripped from her hands.

Dazed but uninjured, she lay on the sidewalk, her head throbbing, but nothing else hurting. She didn't see who hit her. He was gone in an instant.

"My camera!" she said looking around as she slowly got upright. Standing in the rain she turned a complete, slow circle which made her dizzy, but there was no one around.

"Those would have been good shots," Melody bellowed, stomping her foot in a puddle, angry as a child. "Ow," she mumbled as she touched the lump on her head and shuddered from being drenched and cold. That made her head hurt even more. Should she tell the cops? Report a stolen three hundred dollar camera ripped off while alone on McMannus Street?

Madder than a willful toddler, Melody got back in her car, slammed the door closed, and buckled her seat belt.

Stuart would be furious at her for going where it wasn't safe. She hadn't mentioned her nearly rabid interest in photography nor shared her first batch of homeless photos with him. Nor could she bring herself to do so. He'd never understand her new passion.

As soon as she turned north into Scottsdale the sun was out and the streets were dry. Did it only rain on the down and out in Arizona?

Stuart's car wasn't there when Melody pulled into the garage. That was a relief.

She stripped off her wet clothes in the laundry room and put them right into the wash machine, then stark raving nude she walked into the kitchen and took two aspirins before going to her bedroom to shower away the events of the day. She turned on the hot water and examined her pupils closely before getting in. Equal and reactive. Good. Most likely no concussion. The bump on her head still hurt, especially when she washed the sidewalk gunk out of her hair. The hot water and perfumed soap felt wonderful. She stayed there soaking up the cleansing heat and breathing in steam until the hot water tank was emptied.

"Do not fall asleep," she reminded herself as she dried her squeaky clean hair. Not after a bump on the head.

She went back to the kitchen to put an ice pack on her head and spotted a note Stuart had left on the kitchen table saying he'd gone to his wilderness survival class, and would be back in a couple hours, although it didn't say what time he'd left. It could have been two hours ago. Melody had completely forgotten about Stuart's survival class. He had tried everything to persuade her to take lessons with him, but Melody wasn't a fan of climbing around rocks and snakes or sleeping anywhere but a nice clean bed.

Stuart seemed to be happy now and Melody was not going to obsess over his activities any more than she already had. Putting your life on the line in extreme sports had to be some male thing. Probably an over forty male thing. Maybe threatening life and surviving was a necessary stage in male maturation. Stimulating the psyche. An exercise necessary to the healthy well being of type T thrill seekers or type A controllers.

Stuart had tried to explain to Melody the rush of excitement he had felt facing down fears on more than a few occasions.

"Call me a weenie," she'd responded, "but I'm not interested in physically challenging sports just for the sake of taking your breath away while watching the possibility of instant death greet you in the face."

Melody made it a point to stay out of danger, except for her forays into homeless streets with a purse or expensive camera, she admonished herself. Marisa already told her that it might be the same kind of excitement Stuart was seeking and she felt a little better. For the first time she understood and even felt a bit of a bond with Stuart's need for adventure, even though deep down she worried that their separate interests might be leading them further and further apart.

At that moment Stuart walked in from the garage, dirty as a stray dog, a large grin on his face.

"You've got to come with me next time, Melody. This is the greatest!"

"Ow!" Melody said as he put his arms around her.

"Wha'd I do?" Stuart asked, backing away.

"I bumped my head getting into the car carrying boxes from my office. I was just getting some ice to put on it" Melody was shocked at how easily the lie came to her.

"Are you okay? Do you need to get your head examined?" Stuart joked as he draped his arm around her shoulder and walked hip to hip with her to the freezer.

"On the contrary. I think you need your head examined for chasing after danger," Melody chided. Immediately she felt a wave of guilt realizing that's exactly what she'd been doing.

11

Small muffled whispers and bubbling giggles followed by a loud "shhhh" drifted into the living room where Melody and Stuart had settled in for the evening. Melody smiled with delight at Marisa's kids' bedtime chatter.

Stuart grimaced.

"How long are these kids going to be here?" Stuart quietly asked Melody, his irritation evident in his hushed, brusk tone of voice.

"I don't know how long." Melody was quickly jerked out of her reverie by Stuart's impatient tone. "As long as Marisa needs to be in St. Louis. Her father-in-law's in the hospital with pneumonia, Stuart. Be a little patient."

Marisa had called four days ago anxious and distressed and asked if Eric and Josh could stay with Melody and Stuart so she could be with Grant's parents.

"Of course. Pack 'em up and bring 'em over." Marisa had been adjusting quite well in her new roll as single parent. Her boys were delightful, well mannered kids, as close to family as Stuart and Melody had within a thousand mile radius.

Melody had tucked them both into bed in the guest room about twenty minutes earlier and experienced an extraordinary rush of tenderness with every hug and kiss from the two freshly bathed, clean smelling, young boys. Listening to the childish chatter the siblings shared left no doubt in her mind that being a mom someday was an uncompromising need.

Surely, deep down, Stuart was enjoying the boys' stay at their house nearly as much as she was.

"The kid's aren't a problem, Stuart. I've enjoyed having them here, haven't you?"

"No. I haven't enjoyed having them here." Stuart answered in a loud whisper. "No," he reiterated after the slightest pause giving himself another moment's serious consideration. His eyes resembled gray granite as he took Melody's hand. "I'm happy to help Marisa, but I miss our privacy."

No matter what, Melody enjoyed having Eric and Josh stay with them. For the past four days she had picked up the boys every day after school, and thoroughly enjoyed listening to them talk about school friends and teachers over cookies and treats they'd made together.

However, neither their laughter nor innocence appeared to change Stuart's attitude. Their toys left in the living room, however, did have an impact on him. After a snide remark about their invasion, Melody was careful to remove all traces of their play.

Melody was spinning in the vortex of a conundrum — facing choices that were more significant than anything she'd ever had to deal with in her life, and coming up with no solution she could live with. Although Stuart had been ornery and self absorbed lately, she loved him deeply and passionately.

Now there was no hiding the essential difference that Melody didn't know existed and that Stuart had expected Melody to take in stride. Melody and Stuart could live a loving, but childless life together. Or....

Every time Melody even had a flash of considering life without Stuart, it was unbearable. And every time she thought of life without children, it was equally unendurable.

The next morning while in the kitchen scooping coffee into the coffee pot, Melody heard one of the boys call out to her.

"Melody, I need you," Josh sang from upstairs in a squeaky little falsetto morning voice. Melody brightened.

"I'm coming," she sang heading up the stairs.

Josh stood in the guest room, dressed for school with half his shirt tucked in and half out, his hair combed to some extent and shoes on but untied.

"I need a hug," he blurted out as he stretched out his little arms, wiggling his fingers with anticipation.

Melody nearly melted. "Oh, Josh, I'll give you a dozen hugs and an extra squeeze."

Josh put his arms around Melody's neck and squeezed until she could barely breathe. Then he stepped back and nodded. "Thanks, I needed that." And with that he sat down to tie his shoes as if nothing special had happened.

"Where's your big brother? Maybe he needs a hug, too."

"He's in the bathroom. I already gave him one."

"Eric, get going or you guys'll be late for school. Peanut butter and jelly sandwich okay for lunch?"

"Yeah. Smooth peanut butter, please." Eric was eight and in third grade, polite as a first child, and somewhat quiet. He looked just like his father, and had inherited the kindness of his mother. One day he'd have girls falling all over him. Right now he was still missing his father.

With his mother away and his grandfather in the hospital, Eric was troubled, although he was doing a good job of trying to hide his feelings. How in the world does a boy so young learn he's supposed to be brave when facing loss? He was being protective of Josh and that seemed to be good for both of them. Melody had called his teacher to let her know what was happening in Eric's life.

Melody got the kids buckled up in the car, and drove them to school—only about five minutes late. "Sorry guys, I'm still new at this. Tomorrow, we'll be on time for sure."

"When's my mom coming home?" Eric asked.

"I don't know yet. Let's call your mom after school today and see how your grandpa's doing, okay?"

The phone call after school proved to be good news. Grandpa Fisher was fine, but weak, and would be released from the hospital tomorrow. Marisa was staying a couple more days to make sure the elderly in-laws were fine on their own, then she'd head back to Scottsdale.

12

For the first time in his life Stuart was worried about his relationship with Melody. He was certain she loved him deeply and completely as he did her. He would die of a broken heart if she ever stopped loving him. But the old problem of kids had begun brewing once again with the Fisher boys in the house.

"I'll give Melody more love and happiness than any child could ever bring. I swear I will." He took a deep breath. "She's the love of my life," he acknowledged to himself. "She'll get over this."

More than anything at this very moment Stuart wanted to show Melody his love for her in a spontaneous orgy of passion and tender love making. He even picked up the phone, then realized that wasn't a possibility, nor even a good idea.

"Timing, Stuart. Don't forget timing," he reminded himself. He would need to be extra patient and loving. Understanding and exciting. A smile crept over his face at the thought of all that they had together.

"She'll get over this," he repeated to himself.

Still, this was a work day, with deadlines and appointments as though today were any normal day in Stuart Fox's personal life.

Stuart looked at his appointment calendar, and tenderly tucked away thoughts of Melody.

"Today's Tuesday." Every hour on the page of his desk calendar was filled with appointments, deadlines, and notes in the margins with names of people whose calls he needed to return. "Tuesday. 10:00. A meeting with the Arizona Tourism Board," he read silently off the page in front of him. "Oh, good, one of my remaining good clients. We're supposed to go over copy for their new magazine ad."

He dialed the copywriter's extension. "Mimi. Have you got the copy finished for the tourism ad?" It's a little late to be asking, Stuart realized. He should have been on this yesterday.

"Copy's done. Layout's done. You looked at it and approved it yesterday. In fact you loved it. It's on your desk. No?" Mimi asked with surprise. "You want me to print out another copy for you?" She was a bright and clever copywriter. Talented and not one bit overwhelmed by deadlines. In fact Mimi was one of the agency employees, like Grant had been, who thrived on deadlines, the tighter the better.

"Oh, here it is. Thanks. I've got stuff on my mind." Shit, he thought as he hung up, angry that even a little personal blip slipped out of his normally contained thoughts. His private life was nobody's business.

12:00. Ad Federation luncheon meeting. "Have to go." The luncheon would give Stuart a chance to show his agency's strength just by his confident presence, which would have to be a superb performance today based on the way he was feeling. Hopefully he could stop the nasty rumors circulating about his agency's premature death. After Grant's heart attack, rumors had cropped up faster than weeds on a newly tilled garden. Putting a stop to rumors among the advertising community was tantamount to making gold out of lead, but some things were important enough to keep pursuing. Like Melody. Anyway, he usually enjoyed Ad Fed meetings, schmoozing with old friends and listening to gossip as long as it was about other agencies. He would shore up relationships with people, visit with other agency owners and staff and possibly meet a regional marketing director on the lookout for an exceptional ad agency—just like Fisher and Fox. "You never know," Stuart, ever the optimist, said to himself. Latching on to one of those gems would certainly turn around this melancholy day. It could bolster the long range viability of the agency.

Stuart had talked to Sean Riley, a print rep with whom he had a strong business relationship even though Sean was nearly young enough to be his son—a fact that irked Stuart. Sean had recommended Stuart's agency as a perfect match to Gary Appleby, the marketing director of a new golf resort and residential development company about to be built in Scottsdale.

Sean Riley had invited Appleby to the luncheon as his guest so he and Stuart could meet and talk informally. Stuart certainly could use a new client, although he'd never have admitted that to anyone. It would be as important for his ego as for his company's financial well being. The agency's bottom line remained healthy thanks to the Scottsdale Anti-Aging Clinic, but Fisher and Fox was still dangerously dependent on that singular account. Stuart was determined to change that—as soon as he found the time.

2:00. A staff meeting that Stuart was unprepared for.

3:00. Appointment with Greg Parker and Jeff McGonagle, the Anti-Aging Clinic's marketing director and the CEO.

Stuart picked up the phone again to call Melody, then put it down. Any more thoughts of Melody and their differences had to be shoved away, disregarded until later. He couldn't let his personal life sabotage business. There was plenty of time to think about Melody, but not today—not during business hours anyway.

Stuart and Greg Parker always scheduled their meetings for the end of the day to relax a little and yet be sure to have enough time for details that needed going over. This meeting was set up specifically to discuss expanding their regional coverage. Just the thought of the opportunity made Stuart's creative juices flow faster. This was a far better opportunity than the dog food company's commercial he and Grant had produced that brought them their first moment of fame. However, the past never counts in the advertising business. The good as well as the bad are often forgotten as soon as the next star began to shine. Fickle business. This campaign, hopefully, would bring Fisher and Fox fortune as well as fame.

For an instant Stuart was again plagued with loneliness for Grant. Grant had gotten them this anti-aging account. It was Laurel, Stuart's first wife, who had called Grant and told him about the possibility of the clinic as a good account. She had some connection with the clinic Stuart couldn't remember. He owed Laurel more than he was comfortable with. Stuart didn't like owing anybody any favors. Especially his ex-wife.

A small thought pierced Stuart's consciousness and kept growing closer and larger, like a tumbleweed blowing toward him from miles away. The disturbing thought he couldn't disregard was what if, perhaps, there really could have possibly been any reason, any at all, for Grant's heart attack other than natural causes like Melody thought.

"No. Absolutely not. That's nonsense. You can't cause a heart attack. And who would have wanted Grant dead anyway? Nobody in the world."

The clinic's success was phenomenal. Maybe it was the timing, maybe it was the location, maybe it was the doctors. Maybe it was Stuart's brilliance, of course. Dr. Shepard, the medical director, was receiving and enjoying glorious accolades from various trade publications. Sawyer Wiles, the clinic's chief financial officer was silently enjoying looking at the numbers as only accountants can delight in. His strict fiscal policies were creating profitability during a period of growth which he considered a brilliant financial feat, indeed. The research grants awarded to the lab had been a great financial coup. That was Eva Blackwell's doing. The researchers at the clinic were close to finalizing results on drug tests with rats that would be portentous to the future of anti-aging medicine and therefore to the cost of medical care for the elderly. Eva was already salivating over the personal ramifications of the publication of those findings.

A local ten o'clock news anchor was one of a few prominently visible clinic patients. Not only did his looks and attitude change to that of a man ten years younger, the improvement in his vitality was instantly discernible by even the most discriminating critics. Yes! Win-win for everyone involved. His face lift hadn't hurt his overall younger look, either. It was hard to measure how many of the clinic's new clients were the direct result of the anchorman's publicly attributing his rejuvenation to the Scottsdale Anti-Aging Clinic. It certainly was priceless public relations.

Stuart wondered how Melody would feel if he signed on for treatment. Anything to put off the dreaded, debilitating effects of aging. He could make it a business expense and legitimately so. It would be beneficial. No, it was more than that—it was imperative to understand exactly what it feels like to be a patient, and how it feels to be rejuvenated by ten years. It would help in planning market strategies to have a personal experience. Maybe they'd both do it. "How young would I look?" he began to ponder. "Thirty two? Late twenties? How young would I feel?

After Stuart was examined, tested, questioned, poked, and prodded, he was given an array of nutritional compounds and supplements to take daily including vitamins, herbs, extracts, minerals, and hormones. These were all specifically calculated and formulated for his body, age, nutrition, and state of his overall health. Herbs like vinpocetine and ginkgo biloba were prescribed to enhance brain activity. Various compounds were prescribed specifically for their antioxidant benefits like acetyl L-carnitine, phosphatidylserine, vitamin C, vitamin E, and Alpha lipoic acid to keep free radicals from their degenerative effects.

Some compounds were added to the list for healthy heart functioning including CO Q10 and creatine monohydrate. Others were intended to benefit joints and cartilage functioning for agility and flexibility. These included Hawthorn berry extract, glucosamine, a little boron, and S-adenosylimethionine. More specific recommendations were prescribed for hormone replacement therapy including DHEA, testosterone, very carefully monitored, and chaste berry extract. L-arginine was prescribed to be taken thirty minutes before sexual activity. Of course, the B vitamins, and various omega fatty acids were included in his mix. Soy, zinc, and especially manganese, necessary for the production of the ultimate antioxidant enzyme, superoxide dismutase were mandatory. The medications were all provided by the clinic and packaged in daily dose units—the only way to keep track of the complicated concoction.

These were all in addition to a nutritionally charted diet and Stuart's own personal physical exercise program. Stress reduction exercises were compulsory since no combination of ingested additives could ever overcome the damage done to a body by continuous stress. Short, non-business stress related retreats were highly encouraged.

Stuart felt physically at the top of his form. His conviction of the clinic's ability to reverse the aging process—or at the very least to slow it down—was as strong as a missionary's faith in Jesus.

The only part of the whole program Melody embraced was the suggested stress reducing frequent get aways.

13

"Hey, Marisa, Hi. I haven't seen you in ages," prattled a petite blond woman who recognized Marisa in the check-in line at Sky Harbor International Airport. She ignored Melody.

"Laurel, hey. I'm just fine. Where're you headed?"

"Mexico. Scuba diving for a few days."

Melody wanted to become invisible and let the two old friends gab about whatever. Running into your husband's ex-wife was something Melody could have lived without. Running into your husband's ex-wife on her way to play in the same paradise as your husband's fantasy vacation was an event Melody certainly did not include on her list of things-to-do-before-I-die.

"You know Melody, don't you? We're headed for Atlanta." Marisa was cool and comfortable face to face with two Mrs. Stuart Foxes who had never met before.

"Hi," was all either of them said after a half beat of silence. The nonverbal conversation was much more intense. Laurel was silently arrogant. Melody nodded courteously, biting her tongue. She didn't understand her instant bad attitude toward Laurel since Laurel was the one Stuart dumped. Melody knew without a whit's hesitation that she was unquestionably the Mrs. Fox who was the love of Stuart's life. Melody smiled a saccharine smile.

Melody's curiosity about Stuart's less than nine month marriage to this — she hated to admit it — this gorgeous woman was piqued to overload. Why had he moved out of Melody's apartment, married Laurel within months, and then divorced his new wife after less than a year of marriage? Stuart wouldn't talk about that. He would only say he married Laurel without realizing he had remained in love with Melody. He told Melody that leaving her then had been the biggest mistake in his life, and he was eternally grateful that she'd been willing to talk to him again, let alone see him after he'd stupidly married someone else.

A year after they had parted, they met again by chance on board a flight from Chicago to Phoenix which Stuart declared proved they were destined to be together forever.

The plane to Atlanta was full. After Marisa answered all Melody's questions about Laurel, the friends talked about where they would go, what they wanted to eat, what they wanted to shop for, and looked through the flight magazine, comparing restaurant ads in the Atlanta area. They were both excited about their just-us-girls get away.

Marisa sat in the middle seat, not complaining. Melody hated the middle and was happily hunkered down in the aisle seat. The woman across the aisle was sound asleep before the plane left the tarmac, softly snoring. An hour into the flight she woke up and stared at Melody with eyes so yellowish-brown they were strangely cat-like. She looked piercingly, quizzically, at Melody for a long time. It was most invasive and slightly bizarre, Melody thought.

"Be careful what you do with what you find young lady," the woman began out of nowhere, speaking in an accent Melody couldn't place. "Stay out of it. It's ugly. If you don't, you could be next."

"I beg your pardon—," Startled, Melody looked curiously at this eccentric woman. She tried to be considerate, speaking as if she was talking to an elderly, confused, lonely woman. Could this odd old woman have some kind of psychic ability? Could she sense something about Melody and could her message have anything to do reality? Of course not, Melody chided herself. "Next?" That's what the note she'd found in her office had written on it. "Are you talking to me?"

"You know I am," the woman hissed.

"I don't understand." Melody's pulse began racing. This was too weird, even for a psychologist who'd seen many, many weird, sick patients. Maybe this woman was one of the schizophrenics going to the schizophrenia conference.

"Be careful young lady. The sky is about to fall," the old woman whispered in her thickly acented English.

"I'll be very careful. Thank you." She tried not to snicker or sound condescending while some intrinsic part of her felt compelled to heed the woman's advice.

"Don't laugh at me!" the strange lady snapped.

Melody took a quick breath to collect and compose herself. "I'm sorry. It's just...uh...well...you surprised me. The sky is falling?" Melody felt like playing along.

"Never mind. I can see you aren't a believer. Just remember this: not everything is what it seems." And with that the woman shut her eyes, folded her arms, and leaned back in her seat.

"I have to agree with you there. Couldn't agree more," Melody said under her breath. A shiver ran down Melody's spine.

One yellow eye popped open and looked at Melody malevolently but nothing more was said between the two of them the rest of the flight.

"Check out this lady across the aisle," Melody whispered to Marisa. "I'll tell you about her later."

Marisa leaned forward, ostensibly to put her magazine back in the pocket of the seat in front of her while sneaking a long look to her left. She looked back at Melody and rolled her eyes. "Tell me now!"

"Not 'till we're off the plane."

While Melody was at the conference, Marisa went gallery hopping to check out the Atlanta arts scene. She was hoping to find someone whose talent she could discover at a reasonable price and recommend to her gallery. This would be a tax deductible trip for her too then, not just Melody. And possibly the beginning of a reputation for excellent buying skills. It was going to be a long, exhausting, sore feet, exhilarating day.

Marisa was psyched, but her energy had been zapped by a fitful night's sleep. She hadn't been able to sleep after Melody told her the uncanny warning from the woman across the aisle on their flight. She replayed what Melody had repeated to her over and over and came to the conclusion the woman was obviously bonkers.

Marisa spent nearly six hours walking the arts district searching for the next undiscovered Picasso. Or Chihuly. Or Goodacre. She took one break for lunch and another for coffee, talking to store owners and artists, evaluating vessels of glass, pottery, and paper; water colors, oils, and mixed media paintings; bronze, stone, and iron sculptures, and noted how each gallery displayed their art work. She picked up business cards and post cards representing artists she believed would sell well in Scottsdale. Tomorrow she'd start at the Art Institute in Buckhead. After a full day she headed back to the hotel, jazzed with what she'd seen but tired to the bone.

Marisa rifled through her suitcase looking for the fingernail glue she'd dropped in a plastic bag and stuffed in her suitcase at the last minute in case of a finger nail emergency. Finally, after messing up everything she'd carefully pressed and packed, she remembered. "Ah, I put the glue in the side zipper pocket in case it leaked." She unzipped the zipper and reached in. There was something there beside the plastic bag. It was a small envelope, like the kind extra buttons come in attached to new clothes. Curious, but unconcerned, she took out the envelope.

She could tell immediately that the envelope didn't hold buttons. By the feel, the contents were more like old sinus capsules. When had she last used the suitcase, she wondered as she opened the envelope and, to her surprise, poured seven white capsules into the palm of her hand. "I never put those capsules in there," she said at last. "I've never even seen those capsules before. Grant used this suitcase last." Her mind stopped working, frozen with wonder. Just then she heard a click as Melody slid her plastic key in the lock.

"Melody—" Marisa's voice was shaky and faint. "Melody, come over here. Look at this," she said as her friend came in.

Slowly Marisa peeled back her fingers, revealing the seven capsules.

"What are they?" Melody asked.

"I don't have any idea." Marisa was white as a ghost.

"Where'd you get 'em?" Melody asked.

"Melody, I found these in the pocket of my suitcase. I didn't put them there."

"And—" Melody said.

"Grant used this suitcase last. I don't remember exactly when or where he went."

Melody picked up one of the pills and looked at it carefully. There were no manufacturer's markings. No indications at all, from what Melody could see.

"Magic beans?" Melody replied in an attempt at levity. Could Grant have been taking drugs without his wife and closest friends knowing Melody wondered to herself. Of course. People taking drugs don't broadcast it.

Melody tried to be calm and cautious. She didn't want to upset Marisa any more than she already was, but these pills might answer a lot of previously unanswered questions. An overdose? Coke? Did any of the ER doctors or nurses even look for a drug reaction in the emergency room?

"Was he sick, Marisa?"

Marisa silently shook her head.

Melody finally asked the question that stuck in her throat like a dry cork. "Grant wasn't into drugs, was he?" Melody put her arm around Marisa's shoulder as they sat on the edge of the bed.

"I don't believe he was, Melody. It's way too out of character for him." Was it possible Marisa thought to herself. No. But then, neither was it possible for him to be fine and dandy one minute and dead the next. "I can't believe he would have ever gotten into drugs. I just can't."

"I know there are at least two guys at the agency that do drugs. I can assure you, it goes on in lots of places Marisa, especially creative places with a lot of stress."

"No. He couldn't have been," Marisa responded with a meager surge of positive memories. "Remember, he was into vitamins and all that health stuff after he got the Anti-Aging account."

The Scottsdale Anti-Aging Clinic. Melody was horrified by the thought that Marisa's statement could lead to something nearly beyond comprehension in its vileness. It was a long shot, but it could be the connection that finally made everything fall into place. A possibility she hoped and prayed wasn't true for many reasons.

They looked at each other in silence, alarm rising slowly, both women trying to deny that the clinic could have had anything to do with Grant's death.

Every sound in the room became exaggerated during their shocked silence. A siren's wail blared a cautionary foreboding as it approached and then passed under their hotel room window. Muffled conversation and impulsive laughter in the hall seemed to mock the intensity of the electrified air within the room. The motor of the small refrigerator clicked on, startling the two friends out of their immobilization.

"Is there anything in that refrigerator? I think we could both use a drink, just to slow down our imaginations for a minute," Marisa injected into the silence.

"What d'you want? I'm gonna have a vodka."

"I'll have a scotch." Marisa answered.

"I'll go down the hall and get some ice. I'll be right back," Melody uttered.

The door slammed hard and loud behind her, reverberating down the quiet hall. Melody jumped at the noise, thinking it sounded like a gun shot—although she didn't know what a gun shot sounded like in real life.

As she lifted the lid and bent over the ice chest, Melody heard soft, regular footsteps coming toward her.

You could be next…. The accented words spoken by the woman on the plane involuntarily surfaced.

The face of the spooky stranger with the yellow eyes and the scrawled note left on her desk seemed to appear on the wall in front of her, but she knew it was her imagination. She couldn't think of anything else over the slow, steady, increasingly loud footfalls of big feet approaching from around the corner. Her heart began to pound. Fear rose up from her toes to her throat. Would someone find her body thrown in the ice chest by whoever was after her? Who was she next after? How would they have found her here?

Melody finally fought her paralyzing fear and gathered up a bucket of ice, her only weapon, prepared to throw it in the face of whoever was after her. She swung around to face her silent attacker, ice bucket raised.

There stood a short, stocky man with big heavy orthopedic shoes, about seventy-five years old, fringes of silver, curly hair framing his smiling face, standing there politely with an empty ice bucket in his hand. He nodded to Melody. "Did you leave any for me?" he said casually in a thin voice with a thick Southern drawl. "I didn't mean to scare you, honey. Sorry," he continued as he noticed her frightened expression. He scooped up his ice and headed back down the hall without a backward glance.

In the safety of their room the tension eased and she burst out laughing—laughing so hard she had trouble explaining to Marisa what she was laughing at.

"I thought they'd found me—the bad guys the airplane lady tried to warn me about," she managed. "You know—'You could be next'—It turned out to be a friendly little old man filling up his ice bucket. Now I really need that drink."

Marisa took the ice bucket out of Melody's shaking hand.

"The sky is falling." Melody held up her plastic glass as a toast.

"Be careful what you do with what you find," Marisa added, soberingly. "Melody, I'm confused. I'm nearly out of my mind over the thought of Grant having brought this on himself. We loved each other. We never kept secrets. I feel like I'm sinking in a foreign sea. I'm also mad as hell."

"Marisa, slow down. We don't know what's in those capsules. Maybe they're anti-aging meds that really didn't have anything to do with Grant's heart attack. I'm sorry I ever questioned...."

"You didn't start anything. I wondered, too, but I didn't dare talk about it because then it might be real. Now, these pills in his suitcase make everything seem different. I thought I knew him."

"You did. You were a perfect, loving couple. Don't let your imagination get in the way of your wonderful memories."

"Thanks. I hope you're right. Here's to our long lasting friendship," Marisa toasted.

"Friendship," repeated Melody, drinking her scotch too fast, hoping it would help her sleep.

14

During a particularly uninspiring presentation on the history of pharmacotherapy for schizophrenia, Melody's attention was picked up and carried as if on a warm breeze back to when she was a little girl at home with her sister, Eileen. She had a vivid picture frozen in time of Eileen rocking on a chair and not answering the streaming questions Melody was asking her. Melody was suddenly flooded with a childlike sense of failure that she had never been able to help her sister. Should she attempt to find her once again?

Melody decided she'd sneak out of the presentation as soon as she could without too obviously interrupting the lecture. As the speaker took a sip of water, Melody picked up her bag and slunk out the back exit.

It was only eleven on Tuesday morning. Enough time to hit the expo hall, maybe take in a chair massage, hopefully get Eileen off her mind, then go to the luncheon where there was another speaker and still have time to get to the aging and dementia afternoon session. She had listened to enough about schizophrenia.

"Melody? Melody Fox?" a voice questioned from someone

walking toward her. The male voice was familiar but she couldn't place it.

As he got closer, she remembered the face that went with that wonderful deep bass announcer type voice. She remembered meeting Russ or Ross what's-his-name at the Anti-Aging Clinic's opening. Melody was surprised and happy. Now she wouldn't have to make up a reason to call him.

"Russ Daniels," he said as he caught up with Melody and extended his hand. "We met at the Scottsdale Anti-Aging Clinic."

Melody was surprised at her reaction. She felt an unexpected attraction as he approached. She tried to convince herself that the excitement she felt was because of her surreptitious mission to introduce him to Marisa. But she knew her feelings had nothing to do with anyone but the man in front of her.

Very formal, Melody thought as they shook hands. Good. Safe. His hand felt warm, sensual. She'd never felt nearly this electrified by a man's handshake before.

"Russ. Good to see you. How are you?" His light brown hair framed a clean shaven boyish face lit up by a mischievous grin. His frame was slight but masculine.

"Just fine. And you?"

"Fine. What're you doing here?"

"I'm covering the conference for CNN's HealthMatters. You're here for the conference, hm? Heard any news that'll change the future of humanity that needs to be reported to the rest of the country?"

"Not so far, but it's only Tuesday."

"You have time for lunch?" he asked casually.

"Sorry, no. There's a luncheon in less than an hour, but I could go for a cup of coffee," Melody quickly added.

"There's a Starbucks around the corner."

They sat across from each other at a small table. She stretched her arms, rubbed her neck, and began to relax. They talked easily and laughed about nothing while they drank their coffee. Suddenly Melody realized it was only three minutes before the luncheon presentation by Gordon Maxwell, a speaker she'd been particularly keen on hearing. "I better run. I'm going to be late."

"How about dinner tonight?" Russ asked.

"I'm here with..."

"Your husband?" Russ's voice didn't change. "We'll all go."

"No, not my husband..."

"Oh," Russ spoke as if he'd exposed some clandestine rendezvous.

"No, no, no. Nothing like that!" Melody laughed. "I'm here with a recently widowed girl friend. In fact I was thinking of calling you to meet her. You're not married are you?"

"Divorced, and really not ready to meet anyone, Melody, but the invitation still stands. I'd like to take both of you out for dinner tonight."

"What time?"

"Whatever's good for you."

"Eight?"

By the time Melody entered the large banquet hall, most people had already been seated. There were only a few scattered single seats available at the round tables of eight.

Melody had always been fascinated by the psychology of seating. People tend to sit in the same general proximity no matter what the conformity or size of the room. There are those who prefer front and center. Those who always sit in the back. Others left of center, end of a row, or near an exit. Each choice had character traits that accompanied the individual decisions. Melody usually preferred slightly closer than half way to the front, not too far from the end of the aisle, preferably on the right, the speaker's left. She quickly chose a table with six men, one woman, and one empty seat near her preferred position close to the exit. The only inconvenience was going to be that her back was to the podium, but that was the case with all the empty seats. The group at the table had already introduced themselves and the man next to her seemed annoyed at Melody's appearance.

"Damn," he blurted out in a slow, drawn out Southern accent, looking at her. "I was planning on two desserts." Everyone at the table laughed. He winked at Melody with twinkling eyes in a pudgy face.

Usually Melody preferred the company of men to women, but she was afraid she'd misjudged this group. They all seemed to know each other and this made her feel like the odd man out.

"Don't mind Jess. If you offer him your dessert, you'll have a friend for life. I'm Matt Hutton from Norfolk, Virginia. Psychiatrist. The gentle giant next to you is Jess Farmer. He's with American Testing Labs."

"We're into drugs," he drawled, making 'drugs' a two syllable word. "You been to our booth yet?"

"Not yet. I'm Melody Fox from Scottsdale," she said looking around the table. "Psychologist. Unemployed."

Melody was surprised by her instant admission.

Jess put his chubby hand on hers and conspiratorially whispered loud enough to be heard by all "Well, you come work for us, darlin'. We could use a lovely lady like you collecting urine specimens."

"Jess, control yourself." Matt Hutton's friendship and admonishment were both recognizable in his voice.

The other four men and one woman sitting at Melody's table introduced themselves, and she had, indeed, picked a very interesting table. One man was a professor of psychology at the University of Chicago. Another was a psychiatrist in Miami specializing in treating victims of terrorism. The man directly across from her was a sports psychologist who worked with the Atlanta Braves. The remaining man was a neuropsychologist who specialized in infant head trauma. The woman at the table, Phoebe Green, appeared to be in her early seventies, and had been a psychiatrist in various capacities since before most of the group seated at the table had been freshmen in college. Longer than Melody had been alive. Phoebe's eyes were gray, the same light gray as her hair, and they looked at Melody with as much concern as a life long friend. "You must still have some interest in psychology or you wouldn't be here, child, am I right?"

"I'm just burned out. I'm slightly bored by the whole clinical thing. One of the reasons I came to this conference was to get re-energized—find a new focus."

That seemed to please Phoebe.

In a few moments lunch was served and conversation lapsed. The host of the Southeast Psychological Association gave a few words of welcome and thank you's just as desert was being served.

"Here Jess, take my desert. Please."

"Why, thank you my dear. I promise to do you a favor in return some day."

By the time lunch was over they had all exchanged business cards which would be filed away and likely forgotten. Maybe not.

Gordon Maxwell's talk proved to be less inspirational than Melody was primed for, but the table companions had been above expectations.

Melody skipped the last of the schizophrenia symposium and attended the aging and dementia session. The speaker was dynamic and a wonderful presenter. Some of the information concurred with things Stuart had told her, but the conclusions differed greatly. The only outcome that seemed undisputed was that aging is still inevitable, though life expectancy has been increased more in the last hundred years than in the previous thousand years. More of that was due to reductions in infant mortality than life extension. The social issues of fulfillment and productivity, isolation and abuse, and the financial impact on society of aged seniors living a much extended life span were all touched on during the session. Melody was fascinated.

Stuart wouldn't agree with any of this, Melody thought. The Scottsdale Anti-Aging Clinic had unquestionably converted him to a rabid believer.

Anti-aging had become another arena in which she and Stuart would never share common ground.

In their hotel room late that afternoon Marisa talked on and on about her fabulous artistic discoveries, as if she wanted to prevent any space for further discussion of the seven white capsules to be allowed to intrude. Nonetheless, each of them seemed to be waiting for the other to bring up the subject, expectations lingering in the air like smoke.

"I just want to relax tonight, if that's okay with you," Marisa said as she flopped back on her bed. "Something good to eat, maybe room service, something to drink, and no walking around."

"I've kind of made other plans for us for tonight."

"Oh yeah? You have?" Marisa quizzed, with a smile on her face.

"You'll enjoy this evening. I promise."

"What?."

"I ran into Russ Daniels in the hotel lobby today. I don't remember if I ever mentioned him to you," Melody slipped in as casually as she could manage.

"Who is he?"

"A guy I met at the Anti-Aging Clinic's opening after you left that night. He's a health reporter for CNN and he's covering the conference."

Marisa looked at her with one blonde eyebrow raised.

"We had coffee this morning and he invited us out for dinner. I said yes. He's fun. You'll enjoy him."

"My guess is he's single and you're trying to be a matchmaker. Am I right?"

Melody managed a guilty expression while smiling a smile that asked for forgiveness, all at the same time.

"You don't have to like him. It'll be a fun evening, though. He's recently divorced and not ready to look for someone, so we'll all just go as friends, okay? By the way, Eva from the Scottsdale Clinic was mentioned favorably by the doctor who gave a presentation on aging this afternoon. I've got to call Stuart and tell him."

Melody dialed, got the answering machine, and left a brief message. "He's probably still at the office. I can call him later," Melody said, turning to Marisa.

The Atlanta Fishmarket Restaurant sported a giant pink fish sign hanging outside so no one could miss it. The bar was crowded with diners waiting for a table. The smells of garlic, chili, butter, and other aromatic flavors mingled into a mouth watering melange that made stomachs growl.

"Mmmm, I want whatever it is I'm smelling," Marisa said, watching a waiter pass by with a tray carried high on his shoulder, piled with four delicious looking dishes.

Russ was definitely not a stranger at this place. Quite a few people stopped by to talk and joke with him while the threesome waited for a table. Russ's looks and demeanor were appealing, especially his mischievous bad boy smile. He was totally comfortable with himself which added to his charisma.

The blackened grouper was wonderfully hot, the pecan crusted red pepper salmon fantastic, and the Margarita marinated grilled halibut superb. The wine, crisp and full. Melody hadn't seen Marisa so animated in ages. It made her feel happy and slightly jealous at the same time — that out-of-character jealous streak again. Russ Daniels had made Melody feel singularly prized until she could see he made Marisa feel the same. He probably made every woman feel exceptional.

Over the last dregs of coffee, Marisa mentioned Melody's photography project to Russ. Russ was impressed by Melody's intention to document the mental state of homelessness.

"You know, that sounds like it could make a powerful documentary. Interesting..." Russ's speech drifted off as he seemed to be working on details of the project already. "Regrettably, we've got a lot of homeless people here in Atlanta."

"I was hoping to shoot some photos while I'm here." The words tumbled out of Melody's mouth.

"Want to shoot some pictures tonight? I'd be happy to show you around the sleazy sections of Atlanta. I'd like to see your work."

There he goes again, Melody thought, making me feel uniquely prized. Excitement surged through her although she tried not to act like a puppy about to go for a ride.

"Actually, I have a new camera with me and I'd love the chance to try it out. I ordered it on line and it came just before we made this trip. Could we go now?"

15

Stuart felt disoriented. Every room in the house seemed to resonate Melody's absence. He'd never been alone in his own house overnight. Stuart felt edgy, displaced. Alone.

On second thought, it won't be so bad, he thought, as he looked around the living room and decided to enjoy the quiet.

Monday morning he made coffee and scrambled a couple of egg whites, poured a glass of orange juice and took his breakfast, his package of pills, and newspaper out to the covered portale overlooking the brilliantly colored garden.

Get over it, he admonished himself when the empty feeling returned. Once he got to the office everything would likely settle into a routine just like every other day. Fisher and Fox still hadn't picked up any desperately needed new accounts. The agency was doing fine on the books, but the Scottsdale Anti-Aging Clinic still remained far too important in the agency's financial balance. The golf resort and residential development account turned out to be nothing. "I'll make cold calls for new business today," he promised while swallowing the last forkful of eggs although he knew he was too overloaded taking care of the clinic account to find the time for scouting.

The one critical component Stuart lacked for successful growth was the ability to let go. To delegate what needed to be delegated. Grant had been far better at that.

It was a typical weekday with a stack of pressing notes and papers that all needed immediate attention. The 'soon' pile, the 'tomorrow' pile, the 'absolutely need today' pile, and the 'hot rush' pile surrounded him. Somehow, nearly everything ended up in the 'today' or 'hot rush' pile. He vowed he'd work harder to keep a little ahead, just like he'd promised every Monday morning. Just like he'd promised to get on the new account search.

Arriving at the agency, Stuart went to the little kitchen behind the receptionist's desk and filled his coffee mug, stopping to say hello to his staff. He needed to know what page everybody was on and routinely made rounds to see his staff in their offices rather than calling individuals into his office. It made for better communication, or at least that's what he believed and it seemed to work. The staff at Fisher and Fox was a close knit group.

Everything seemed to be going along "swimmingly," Stuart's favorite adverb. A word that was not only calming and reassuring, but to him, created an image of an easier era when 'as soon as possible' meant in about a week. Stuart longed for deadlines to slow down, but time doesn't work that way.

"Stuart, Eva Blackwell's here to see you." Annie's message came across loud and clear over the speaker as soon as he was back in his office, jarring him from his nonproductive, contemplative thoughts about the ever quickening pace of time.

Stuart could sense that Annie was annoyed but being polite. Nobody just dropped in on Stuart. Not anyone with the slightest understanding of Stuart's unwritten rules.

Eva had a way of annoying most people and it was obvious that she delighted in that talent. Her flair for churlishness caught people off guard. It was a jolting contrast to her looks. She looked like a perfectly stunning specimen of old wealth and all that goes with it. Actually, that was far from the truth. She had grown up in a dysfunctional family in Peoria, Illinois. No old money except a few dollars hidden by her mother in her underwear drawer.

Eva had picked up her arrogance soon after she developed a body that screamed perfection and she'd learned how to take advantage of it. She'd begun enjoying toying with men at age sixteen. Flirting and manipulating was her double major in college. Microbiology was her minor. She excelled at all three.

"I'll be right out," Stuart said, surprised by Eva's visit.

"Eva. What a pleasant surprise. Welcome to Fisher and Fox. Come on in my office. How about a tour of the place first?" Stuart was slightly unnerved and it showed in his rapid speech, but only if you knew him well — as well as Annie did.

Eva's body language made it quite clear she wasn't really interested in the agency's workings. On the quick tour of the office she lingered outside Grant's office and seemed lost in thought for a moment. Those few seconds seemed in complete contrast to everything Stuart had seen of her behavior up to now. She'd always percolated sensuality, but never sensitivity.

In Stuart's office, Eva slid the chair that was positioned across the desk from him to the side of his desk, so she was closer — a more equal position than seated opposite him. He was unaware of her instinctive leveling machinations. Melody would have caught it in a second.

He began to try to relax although he was still uneasy, wondering if she was there to give him some bad news.

"I'm happy you dropped by."

"I had a few minutes and wondered if I could persuade you to take me out to dinner tonight." She looked him directly in his gray green eyes through long, thick lashes. And she smiled a warm, inviting smile. "Business, of course," she added in counterpoint to what her body was saying. "I've been working every night, and I could use someone to bounce around some ideas with."

Stuart pretended he needed to look at his calendar. Of course he knew he was free for dinner. "Sure. Tonight's good."

Dinner with Eva would be unquestioningly more appealing than eating alone at home. "Where do you want to go?"

"How 'bout Mancuso's?"

"Good. I can pick you up at the clinic or meet you there. What's best for you?"

"I hate walking into a restaurant alone," she lied. "Could you pick me up at my house? It's not far from there."

Do not pick her up at her house, Stuart's inner voice screamed at him. "Sure."

His discomfort and the unexpected surge of electricity at the prospect of having dinner with this beautiful woman fused into a knot of bewitching anticipation. However hard he tried throughout the rest of the day, thoughts of Eva and the evening ahead crept into the work he tried to focus on.

"Just dinner," Stuart spoke lovingly to the photo of Melody on his desk.

That evening Stuart spent longer in his closet choosing what to wear than he'd ever spent dressing for any banquet he'd attended, hosted, or received honors from. He tried to find the balance between not too businesslike and not too casual. After much deliberation, he decided on black slacks and his favorite long sleeve gray Egyptian cotton shirt. Tie? No. Socks? Yes.

Eva's house, like most other houses in the area, was invisible from the street. Stuart's guess from glancing at the outside was that the house was fairly large. He was tense as he drove his Mercedes down her winding drive, flanked on either side by Russian sage in full dazzle and red penstemon peeking through the haze of purple. There was a tall saguaro with three arms and other cactus tastefully arranged to make the entrance inviting. When he got out of his car, Stuart heard the sound of running water — a little stream gurgling among the rocks. It's languid rippling sound was the antithesis of the electricity in his every nerve ending. He hadn't been out with a woman for dinner other than his wife in over five years. Lunch, yeah, that was fine. Dinner? Not quite so routine.

For an instant Stuart felt as skittish as a high school kid picking up his first prom date. He pressed the doorbell and regained his aplomb. He was no school boy, and she was no high school virgin. He was a happily married man who loved his wife dearly, he reminded himself.

When Eva opened the door, he immediately forgot that last thought. This was not meant to be a business dinner.

Eva was dressed in a slip of a silk dress, very plain, very red orange. The contrast with her dark hair, fair skin, and lavender blue eyes made her a stunning specimen of a confident, worldly woman. All five feet four of her.

Heads turned as she walked into the restaurant just ahead of Stuart — quite a reaction for the sophisticated patrons of Mancuso's. It was nothing to Eva. She was used to reactions just like this whenever she deigned it advantageous to turn on her allure. Tonight was one of those nights.

Stuart was not a naive innocent and he enjoyed toying with self assured women. They ordered martinis and sat wordlessly looking at each other while they waited for their drinks. Stuart joined in Eva's sensual game and silently looked into her eyes, which burned with overt desire. The intensity was so gripping that Stuart became uncomfortable. Soon their drinks arrived and they toasted the success of the Scottsdale Anti-Aging Clinic, finally breaking the sensual soundlessness.

Stuart tried to steer the conversation toward business, but Eva derailed his every attempt. Their business relationship was mixed with harmless sexual banter, and they both enjoyed it. Stuart suddenly wondered if he could keep it that way. His body was beginning to undermine his convictions. No more drinks he promised himself. Martinis made him passionate.

Eva appeared more than willing to take their dinner to another level.

"I'd like another martini. How about you, Stuart?" Eva asked, acting demure.

"Fine. Yeah." Definitely NO, he told himself as he motioned for the waiter. But, of course he was not going to be out drunk by a female, especially one as petite and magnificent as she was. He'd just drink his third martini very slowly. Or was this his fourth?

They talked, they laughed, they teased. They ate. They drank. They exchanged inviting innuendoes. It had become an exceptionally stimulating evening.

Driving Eva home, her stolen glances at Stuart's face and crotch while she ran her tongue over her lips could not be mistaken as anything but an invitation for him to join her for more than conversation.

Having an affair was the farthest thing from his mind, however. Having an affair with a client was beyond stupid. Engaging in an affair with a client who was as intelligent, gorgeous, and devious as Eva was unthinkable. But in his martini induced lust he forgot all the reasons why not — he especially forgot the financial dependence Fisher and Fox had in this luscious vixen's company. He was being led by his testosterone right into her lair, and he could hardly wait, desire and anticipation overcoming his better judgment.

They drove silently into Eva's driveway. Stuart kept his eyes straight ahead staring at the garage door, grasping the steering wheel like a drowning man clinging to a buoy, willing himself not to look at Eva. She remained silent, her breathing the only sound in the car. He tried to maintain his resolve not to venture into the land of no return. Suddenly there was no yesterday, no tomorrow. Life's too short.

The red orange dress was off before Stuart had closed the front door behind them. She was enough woman to start a dead man's heart beating again.

In her underwear, Eva grabbed Stuart by the hand and led him to the bedroom. His eyes were glued to her, unaware of anything else. He was mesmerized by her every move. Every nerve ending in his body was on fire, urgently, impatiently waiting for the dance to begin.

She slowly unbuttoned his shirt, taking little licks and nibbles of his skin while his breathing increased. She slid his shirt off while Stuart kissed her deeply, invasively. He moved his lips from her lips to her cheeks to her eyes to her neck while she unbuckled Stuart's belt and unzipped his trousers. He pulled away long enough to tear off his pants, shoes, socks, and shorts. His hands reached out to Eva's shoulders. Softness and warmth contained desire just under the surface of Stuart's fingers. He slid his hands down to remove the remnants of her clothes, exposing her skin to his. They were still standing while he cupped her breast with one hand and explored the other with his tongue.

A blue moon, low and full and huge shined through the sheer draped window, casting shadows across the bed where they fell together, arms and legs entangled, breaths enmeshed. Their sex was rough and hard, just the way Eva liked it. Stuart was blinded and breathless by the intensity of his orgasm, gasping as he came back to earth where chilled air in the bedroom blew over their sweat drenched bodies.

As he lay next to Eva, her head resting on his shoulder while he unconsciously rubbed her back, he knew they were not nearly finished. This was just a break. She was the most sensuous woman he'd ever been with, nearly reaching a climax at his first touch. An eager, playful grin spread over his nearly bruised lips as he relished the remnants of sex. The smell. The steam. The sated breathing. The rudiments of more. He opened his eyes and looked around the room of the woman he'd just fucked and would take again this night before the moon had risen to its zenith. Next time devouring her slowly, deeply.

The room was surprisingly subdued, bordering on stark, and

thus made more revealing by what was not there than by what was. There were no feminine frills, no preppie plaids or Martha Stuart English roses. No photos. No scattered mementos. He could see books piled on her night stand. Text books. Journals. Nothing romantic. In the bathroom, which Stuart could see reflected in the bedroom mirror, were bottles and tubes and brushes, the regalia of feminine grooming, left scattered on the counter top. Eva used those few strewn tools to skillfully enhance her allure.

Stuart closed his eyes and dozed, breathing in synchrony with the rise and fall of Eva's breathing on his chest.

Suddenly he awoke to the sensation of a hand caressing his penis. He responded with an audible moan of pleasure, gently using his hands to explore and tease the body of the woman inciting his senses. Her nipples hardened at his touch. Slowly, their gentle, tender strokes became more heightened, heat and desire building. Stuart slowed again to a dreamy, languid pace, just barely skimming the outline of Eva's body. If Eva wanted to play, she'd picked a perfect playmate, one who could initiate a tidal wave of desire, and yet refrain from crashing. His control was phenomenal. She arched for more, and he again probed deeper and more raptly. As her throaty moans became louder and her lusty response intensified, Stuart again pulled back to barely trace and tease her. When he'd brought her to the pinnacle of passion they shared an explosive, radiating climax.

Then deep sleep overcame them both, still entwined in each other's arms.

Stuart was gone when Eva woke up. She stretched like a cat, called the lab to say she'd be late, and curled up into a ball for another half hour of sleep and dreams. She'd been impressed with Stuart's prowess. He'd do just fine.

"Stuart, how about dinner tonight?" Eva purred over the phone. He'd expected this call all day. Hadn't been able to concentrate on anything at the office because of his anticipation. He'd picked up the phone at least seven times to call her and make sure she couldn't mistake his behavior for anything but an unfortunate drunken mistake.

"Eva, about last night..."

"I know you enjoyed yourself. How about tonight? Do you have any more important plans?"

Stuart seemed to be incapable of saying no to this woman.

"No. No, Eva," he tried anyway.

"Good. Then plan to be at my house around seven."

"More business?" he tried diffusing the conversation as every nerve ending in his body began to tingle and his pulse began to race.

"Whatever you like," she said softly.

Stuart briefly looked around his office as though the phone call was improper.

"No Eva, I..."

"Hmmm?" she purred.

"Pleasure," he responded in a slow, guttural, sexy voice, losing any shred of resistance. He could hear her smile.

"Bring something to my house and we'll have dinner in."

Stuart left right at five o'clock, with the exit remark to those staying late that he was taking work home. He drove up Scottsdale Road oblivious to traffic.

Stuart tried to find something to occupy him until seven o'clock that wouldn't entail going home. All he could come up with was a drink at Buster's. He had two hours to fortify himself.

"Scotch."

When he was a block from Eva's house, primed for a sublime evening of pure sex, he suddenly realized he'd forgotten to pick up dinner. A Chinese restaurant was the first eating establishment he passed as he retraced his route out of Eva's neighborhood.

Eva greeted him with the slightest buss of lips to lips and a smile. She didn't have to work at arousing Stuart's passion. He had no intention of eating the Chinese food before a little play.

He undressed Eva, expressing his hunger for her with every item of clothing he removed. As she headed naked, to the bedroom, Stuart followed, disrobing along the way.

After another round of satisfying sex, they were famished, craving food just as they had craved each other's bodies.

While in the kitchen devouring Chinese take out, they reminisced about how they met, as lovers often do. Then Eva directed the conversation to the clinic.

"So, how are you feeling since you started on the clinic's treatment? You certainly seem to have no problems for your age."

"What do you mean?"

"We're testing this brand new drug that traps free radicals better than anything anyone's worked with before. It's quite promising. Combined with superoxide dismutase, HGH, and telomerase..."

"I love it when you talk technical. It turns me on."

"The results seem nothing short of miraculous. Not only can these chemicals and enzymes slow down aging, they can stall it to a snail's pace. Some subjects seem like they don't age at all."

"Are you telling me you've found the fountain of youth, Doctor? How come we're not advertising it?"

"Because it's still in the animal testing stages. We have to determine the short and long term risks at these levels before going public, but I don't expect any risks at all. It's just a formality. How old do you think I am?" she asked steering the conversation back to more personal issues.

Stuart hated this question. It was a trap any way you looked at it. Damned if you're right, damned if you're wrong.

"Come on, Eva, that's a loaded question. I don't know. How old are you?"

"I'm forty-five." She loved doing this.

Shocked, Stuart was silent with his mouth agog. "You're not. I think you look about twenty-eight."

"I'm forty-five," Eva repeated, her expression dead serious. "That's the truth. How old are you?"

"I'm forty-two," Stuart responded despondently. "I thought I looked pretty young for my age—until now. Am I taking the same stuff you're taking?"

"I can't give you that yet. Not legally," Eva whispered with an amused smile. "As soon as I can, I'll get you some."

16

"I've tried not to think about those damn pills but it's impossible," Marisa said as she and Melody left the shopping mall the next day. "I appreciate your taking time to be with me today. It's not helping. I've just got to talk it out, I think. I'm about to go mad with 'what ifs'." Marisa paused, her eyes searching the sky, the trees, the passers-by for answers that weren't there. "I have to know what they are. I can't pretend they're nothing important. I wish I'd never found them."

"I can get them analyzed easily enough if you want me to."

"I do. I have to know. But I don't want anybody else to know, Melody."

"Ah!" Melody brightened, remembering her luncheon acquaintances from the previous day. "There's this guy I just met at the conference who runs a testing lab. He said he owed me a favor for giving him my dessert. I've got his card and I can ask him. I'll start there." Melody then looked Marisa in the eye. "But you've got to be completely, one hundred percent sure you want to know the results. Once you know, there may be more questions than answers."

"I understand."

The two women walked silently, ending up in front of Sugar's Bakery. "Let's get something to go. Sugar always helps me think better."

"I'd like a slice of chocolate raspberry cheesecake, how 'bout one of those big chocolate chunky chip cookies for you, and a piece of double chocolate mousse cake just in case we need something later."

"Jess Farmer, please."

"One moment please," the operator replied.

"Hello?" the burly voice questioned.

"Jess, this is Melody Fox, your chocolate supplier from lunch. You remember you said you owed me a favor? I've got one. Hate to let a good favor go to waste."

"Boy, you don't waste time, honey," he kidded.

"I have a piece of double chocolate mousse cake in hand. Can you meet me in the lobby?"

"Right now?"

"Well, yeah."

"Give me fifteen minutes."

"That was easy. I'm going to make a quick call to Stuart before I go down." There was no answer, so Melody left a message that she'd call later.

"Sure, I can have this analyzed. That's what we do, sugar. That's no favor," Jess smiled. He had a way of being genuinely personable without ever using a person's given name.

"Well, the real favor is that you tell no one and leave no paper trail," added Melody.

"You sure picked a good one. That's not gonna be so easy, darlin'."

"You didn't say it had to be an easy favor," Melody replied with a grin.

"There's no manufacturer's mark on this." Jess looked at Melody then added, "You know that already," as he continued rocking the capsule back and forth in his beefy palm. "This is one of those health food capsules, probably filled with natural herbal healing stuff."

"You're good at the obvious," Melody said. "I need to know exactly what's in it."

"When do you need an answer?"

"Yesterday."

"Honey, it was just a piece of cake you gave me, not the fuckin' Hope diamond."

"As soon as possible then. Okay?"

"You want me to call you with the results, or how do you want me to handle this top secret case?"

"Call me."

"Okay. Next week then."

Jess raised his eyebrows as Melody handed him the styrofoam box with the cake and her business card with the phone number scratched out and her home number written on it.

"Thanks, for the cake, sugar."

Marisa and Melody tried to make the most of their remaining time in Atlanta. On Thursday they toured two antebellum mansions, visited Olympic Park, and both bought shoes neither of them needed.

While they were back in their room recuperating from a busy but hollow day, the phone rang. Marisa picked it up. "Hello," she said maternally through a growing smile which fell away immediately. "No, this is Marisa. How're you Russ?" She looked directly into Melody's eyes. "Sure, just a minute."

"It's about my photos!" Melody whispered to Marisa, covering the mouthpiece of the phone.

"Okay. Thanks."

"What?" Marisa asked as Melody danced around the room.

"Russ showed the photos I took to his producer who wants to show them to someone who may be interested in filming a TV documentary based on my pictures!"

By Friday morning both women wanted to leave for home. So much had changed since Monday. They immediately changed their tickets for a day earlier than planned and checked out of their hotel.

"Just a few daylight shots of Spring Street and then to the airport, okay? We've got time."

"It would be useless to try to stop you. Let's go."

Friday. One more evening with Eva before Melody came home. Stuart thought about finding an advertising convention where he could take Eva and they could spend more nights together. It was going to be difficult to continue seeing her with Melody home, and not being with her was out of the question. He knew it was stupid and dangerous. He still loved Melody.

His daydreams were suddenly interrupted by the ringing of the phone.

"Hey, Stuart—Marisa and I decided to come home early. I'm calling from the plane. We've had it with being away. We'll be in at 9:55. Can you pick us up?"

"Sure," Stuart's voice cracked. He was consumed both with guilt over having betrayed Melody and disappointment over losing his last night with Eva.

"Stuart, you won't believe this, but one of the cable networks might make a documentary based on some photos I've taken! I'm jumping the gun, but I'm so excited I can hardly believe it," Melody blurted out.

"What photos?" Stuart asked as they embraced.

"You know I've always been interested in photography. I've been taking pictures of homeless people. I ran into Russ Daniels at the conference. We all had dinner together, Marisa, Russ, and me, then he drove us to a place to take some pictures in Atlanta."

"That name's familiar," Stuart said with a puzzled look on his face.

"Russ Daniels, CNN HealthMaters reporter we met at the Anti-Aging Clinic opening."

"That's great," Stuart responded, thinking of how he might use the CNN HealthMaters contact to get positive coverage for the clinic.

"Russ thought the pictures captured some intensity and insight into human suffering that hasn't ever been captured before and he showed them to his producer."

Stuart immediately thought of Melody back in Atlanta as his ticket to time with Eva again. "Melody, that's great," he replied with a smile.

17

Melody's large portfolio of photos was carefully stowed on the rack above her seat. She had been surprised and pleased by Stuart's enthusiasm when she told him about going to Atlanta to talk to CNN about a documentary based on her pictures. She also felt guilty that she was glad he wasn't able to go with her. Now she was on her way to meet with Stan Knight—and Russ. There was something about seeing Russ again that made Melody even more nervous than the prospect of negotiating a contract with CNN. She was unquestionably drawn to him, but so were many other women, she was sure. That's a quality that makes him a successful journalist—his magnetism, both on camera and off, she reasoned as she got off the plane at Hartsfield Airport.

"Melody Fox, please pick up the nearest white courtesy phone. Melody Fox."

She smiled broadly. While in a strange place she could reinvent herself as a successful star, if only for a few minutes. She straightened, head high, swinging her portfolio, and glided to the phone as if she were used to being fawned over for her excellence in—whatever—it didn't really matter.

"This is Melody Fox," she said, self assurance in her voice.

"It's Russ. I'm here at the airport. Knight sent me over to pick you up. Where are you?"

"I'm on my way to ground transportation. Where're you?"

"I'll meet you there in a couple minutes. Are you ready for this meeting?"

"Not really."

"You'll do fine."

On the contrary. Knight had been called away on other business and sent his assistant to meet with Melody. Russ promised to raise hell at the insult, but Stan Knight had given this kid, Jeremy Jones, the authority to make a decision and he was making the most of what would be his short lived hour of power.

"We're just not interested in that kind of project right now. Too negative. Nothing in here to justify our time and investment," he stated flatly as he flipped through the pages of photos. "The images are good, but there's no documentary here. Maybe a gallery'd be more appropriate." He closed the portfolio and slid it across the table to Melody. He then stood up, extended his hand, and offered "Good luck to you," while shooting Russ a look that indicated Russ was way out of his element for even thinking that an on-air newscaster might recognize what would make a good documentary.

"I'm sorry Melody. That guy wouldn't know…"

"Oh—don't, Russ. Please. I shouldn't have expected anything more. I'm not completely discouraged, but I think he's right. My photos aren't meant for TV. Thanks for your help and words of encouragement, but this is not my league."

"Of course it is. Don't let that asshole discourage you."

"I'm devastated, but just for now. I'll get over it. Whether I do anything with these or not, I have this fundamental drive to continue exposing the plight of forgotten street people."

"How 'bout some junk food and a drink to forget about this whole episode?" he asked.

Seated in the noisy pizza parlor, Russ held up his beer glass. "To your first rejection and your future success."

Melody clinked glasses and drank her Chardonnay wondering what the future held for her. If no longer a psychologist, maybe an unrecognized, never famous photographer?

They spent their meal picking on Jeremy Jones' stupidity unendingly, laughing over made-up hurdles he would have to face in his life, laughing over simple stories, and Russ' tales of his incorrigible youth.

At eleven o'clock, alone in her hotel room, Melody called home. No answer. Of course, it's two hours earlier in Phoenix. Stuart's probably still out for dinner. "Hey, Stuart, it's me," Melody said to the answering machine. "Today was not a good day. I got a fast rejection. Like you always say, 'a fast no is better than a slow maybe that eventually turns into no anyway.' I'll be home tomorrow."

The dinner orchestrated by Eva as an intimate prelude to raucous sex included caviar, iced vodka, blinis, and strawberries while the London Symphony Orchestra played Rachmaninov. They kissed each other's fingers, continuing downward to include a few other body parts. Neither said a word, content to let their passions silently build, teasing, tempting, enticing each other while removing clothing, responding to the fiery urge to feel skin against skin. Gasping for air they passionately came together in a fusion of heat, arms and legs wound tightly around each other.

Each time thoughts of Melody attempted to invade Stuart's thoughts, they were immediately cast into the depths of another lifetime.

Melody rolled down her window and breathed in the warm, desert air. "Hi, Stuart," she spoke into her cell phone. "I'm just leaving the airport."

"Sorry about the CNN decision, honey. What're you going to do now?"

"I'm going home first, then out to take more pictures—you know, get right back on that ol' horse."

"Good for you, but be careful. I'll see you tonight."

She loved Phoenix as much as she was beginning to hate Atlanta. She'd had a good time with Russ, but her feelings of rejection were beginning to swell.

After changing into her oldest worn out sweats, Melody picked up her camera and headed downtown. She parked across the street about fifty feet away from the warehouse where she had seen people going in and out. Today she was going to find a spot near the doorway. Maybe she'd find out what was going on inside.

What if I just...go in? she wondered.

Without making a sound she reached the landing where the last three steps made a right turn to the upper floor. It seemed to be one large, cavernous room. Natural light streamed through rows of windows. It looked almost inviting compared to the street. In the middle of the room was a long brown folding table, the kind one rents for meetings or exhibits. Two men were seated on folding chairs facing each other across the middle of the table. One man wore a clean, crisp denim shirt and blue jeans. The other was dressed in a faded flannel shirt and old brown pants. He wore sneakers with holes in each shoe. A toe was visible on each foot. Straggly hair stuck out from the ribbed cuff of a knitted cap. Next to the better dressed man who was obviously in charge were two separate stacks of papers and a stack of short golf score card pencils. On his left was a wooden box.

As Melody eased up the last few steps, two other men came into her line of vision. Two big men. Suddenly three sets of eyes locked on her like a heat seeking missile. Melody instantly turned and ran, jumping the last three steps, barely missing a man in the stairwell. She didn't look back as she reached her car, grabbed the keys from her pocket and hit the remote.

She considered calling the police when she got home. And tell them what? I saw something weird on McMannus Street she thought to herself.

Two days later Melody was on the highway returning home from having her oil changed when the car behind her suddenly raced into the right lane just as she was about to pull over and let it pass on the left. "Stupid driver."

It then slowed down and Melody pulled past but the driver jerked his car into the left lane behind her, following too close. "I'd really appreciate a patrol car right now," Melody yelled at no one.

She was furious and terrified. Smack! The unexpected impact sent Melody's car out of control and it rolled violently upside down as Melody saw earth and sky change places and heard the crashing and smashing of steel and glass. In that instant, she'd rolled completely over and finally landed right side up in the meticulously landscaped median. Melody quickly snapped out of her seat belt and got out, trembling in fear.

Moments later a police car arrived. "Ma'am, you're a very lucky lady," the patrolman said as he shook his head in disbelief. "I've seen real ugly accidents like this where the driver didn't make it."

"Can you call my husband for me please? I'm just too shaky right now."

Stuart was there within ten minutes. "Are you all right?" he asked frantically.

"I'm fine. Just a little shaken. I think the car's totaled," she said as the tow truck arrived.

"I don't care about the car. What happened?"

"This guy ran me off the road — the idiot!"

"Maybe you should go to the hospital just to be sure you're okay."

The next morning, a cloudless sky seemed to reflect promises of good fortune. Although stiff and slightly sore, Melody was bright with optimism and glad to be alive after an accident that could have been fatal. The disappointment of her rejection in Atlanta measured in relation to nearly dying was no more than a blip on her calendar now. The echo of one inept assistant's opinion was actually driving her to hone her talent. As much as it had hurt, he was right. She had a photo essay, not a documentary. But she needed more.

Just this one last session Melody told herself as she headed the rented white Mazda toward McMannus Street.

She was soon parked down the block from the old warehouse. Suddenly she recognized the woman coming toward her.

"Janice? Janice Makowsky. It's me. Dr. Fox. What're you doing here?"

Melody could hardly believe what her former patient had to say.

The next day, still upset by what she had been told, Melody was sitting at her kitchen table organizing photos. Just then the phone rang and she recognized Jess Farmer's gruff Southern accent.

"You sure know how to ask for one difficult favor, young lady," Jess drawled.

"What do you mean?" Melody replied, worry settling over her.

"Although there are some familiar components in this thing, it's not any known combination of drugs. There's meclophenoxate and nootropilan, plus dangerously high doses of DHEA, HGH, and pregnenolone. There's a trace of phenylbutylnitrone which has not been approved by the FDA. There's also MDMA. Definitely illegal. Somebody made this capsule lethal. I've got to report this."

"Not yet," Melody pleaded. "Give me a little time. I've got some ideas."

"You can't keep this hushed up! I've got to report it."

"It could be an experiment by a well respected institution and I need to find that out."

"You're a sly one, little lady. You stay in close touch with me. This is serious, and I could lose my ass keeping this quiet."

"I'll stay in touch. Just give me a little more time to get some vital information. Thanks, Jess."

Out of nowhere the words of the strange lady on the plane to Atlanta gave Melody a chill. "Be careful what you do with what you find." Ridiculous. She was just a little old lady with dementia.

18

Stuart and Melody were celebrating Melody's birthday with a tense, quiet dinner together at Sammy's.

"Will you excuse me a moment," Melody said to Stuart as she got up from the table, briskly walked through the restaurant, and ran outside. She leaned against the cool adobe building and gulped hot, dry air while tears puddled in her eyes.

She struggled to let go of her lingering sadness. Nearly every night now included some horrible disagreement with Stuart. Every day resulted in their growing a little farther apart.

Was there enough love left between them to continue their life together? Or was this where you let go?

One audible, anguished whimper slipped out from her lips as her heart broke. She would always love Stuart in a way, but never the way it had been. Tears flooded over her thick lashes and streamed down her cheeks.

Cut it out! she screamed at herself. She dried her tears and headed for the ladies room to redo her makeup. As she faced her image in the mirror Melody thought about Stuart. How was he feeling about all this? Maybe a little distance would be the best thing right now.

As diligently as he tried to keep thoughts of Eva out of Melody's birthday celebration, Stuart had failed. Waiting for Melody to return Stuart pictured his last night at Eva's and wondered when he'd be able to enjoy the pleasures of her talented fingers once again.

As Melody took her seat, Stuart could tell she'd been crying. She rarely cried, and he felt awful for her deep sadness.

Stuart was flooded with remembered images of earlier, happier days with Melody. Their laughter, their exuberant love making. Their wonderfully happy five years together. If it weren't for her nagging about a child, he surely would never have succumbed to Eva's invitations. Stuart was so easily convinced by his own delusions. His self deception helped settle his stomach and eased his nerves as much as a quart of booze helped an alcoholic.

Yes, he still loved Melody. He would always love Melody. It was just that now he loved Eva, too. He anguished at the thought of losing either of them.

His relationship with Eva had grown significantly in importance to him. She was his first thought when he awoke in the morning, and his last thought when he finally fell asleep. Their affair had upgraded from exploring, devouring sexual partners to familiar, intimate lovers. At least that was Stuart's impression.

Stuart's attempt to hold the Fisher and Fox Advertising Agency afloat was failing. He'd lost another account a week ago and his professional veneer as successful, carefree businessman had become impossible to maintain. The last remaining client other than the clinic was a paltry account that in better days, Stuart wouldn't have even considered taking on. Mitch Long, the manager of Bikes and Hikes Outdoor Gear was a snotty young know-it-all. Stuart had to check his better judgment at the door every time they met to discuss his advertising. Stuart was praying for the day he could tell good old Mitch, 'Fuck you, kid. You don't have a clue.'

In part, the impending demise of the Fisher and Fox agency was due to Stuart's uncontrollable physical desire for Eva. They could only manage to be together during business hours. Time that could have been spent actively acquiring new accounts. But Stuart preferred what he was spending his time getting and wasn't about to give that up.

Having an affair entailed a full web of deceit that Stuart was not well versed in. His contorted reasoning made sense to him, therefore, he assumed, it made perfect sense to Melody. What Stuart didn't count on was the energy it would take to remember his lies and build feasibility on already spoken falsehoods. It was as much work as a full time profession. But he had never counted on falling in love with Eva.

On his way to Eva's one afternoon, with an unparalleled jolt of eagerness to be with her he thought he might be better off without Melody. With Eva, the enchantress.

The 'D' word wouldn't form on his lips, but did squirm it's articulate, suggestive breath into his consciousness. Divorce. Absolutely not. Not unless or until he had no choice. He loved Melody. Stuart knew men who'd had lovers for years. He popped an antacid in his mouth to relieve the now familiar ache in his stomach.

"Eva, Eva," he barely managed to exhale while grasping her wrist to give himself a moment to slow down. Every fiber in his body was gasping for more while she slowly rubbed his erotically responsive skin. Her slick, skillful hands brought him to the brink of ecstasy.

"More?" she asked, her voice full of lust and control.

He sat up and kissed her deeply on the mouth, wrapped her

legs around him, and as soon as she approached her own pinnacle of pleasure, they came together in a slippery, sweaty, climax.

"Stuart, we need to talk." That was always a bad way to start a conversation.

But Stuart pretended not to hear her. Afraid to rerepeat her request, Melody poured herself a glass of Chardonnay and went out into the garden. The evening was warm and still, the neighborhood silent as a vacuum. The balm of nocturnal tranquility was healing and Melody sat there alone, dwelling on good times and bad she and Stuart had shared over the years. A bad case of the 'if-only's' started to overtake Melody in the still darkness, and she wrestled with the thought until she'd successfully convinced herself there were no longer any 'if-only's' to be considered. The end of the happiness she knew with Stuart appeared to be within a breath of the finale.

"Star light, star bright, first star I've seen tonight. I wish I may, I wish I might, have this wish I wish tonight." Wishing on stars was really desperate, she thought. She smiled to herself at the simplicity of wishing on a star and the childlike innocence it took to believe in it.

A horrifying thought struck her as a shooting star, bright and unexpected, fell across the sky. What if Stuart had been given some crazy, experimental drug from the clinic that caused his recent change in behavior?

19

Russ. His name appeared from Melody's subconscious like the answer to a trivia question you didn't know you knew. But this was no trivial matter Melody thought with grave apprehension. She needed someone to help unravel all the bits of information and questions raging through her head about what was happening on McMannus Street.

His card was in her purse in the kitchen. They hadn't spoken since the idea for the homeless documentary was nixed, but she was sure he'd help her. I just hope he isn't in Ghana or Uzbekistan or god knows where investigating some plague or something really important, she prayed silently.

Taking the cordless phone from the kitchen outside into the still warm night, she punched in his number.

"Hello?" came a groggy response after five rings.

"Russ? It's Melody Fox in Scottsdale." Her voice was breathy and nervous.

"What time is it?" he asked.

"Oh, I'm sorry. I guess it's one there."

"You sound strange. Are you all right?"

"I'm okay. I just need to talk to you. Some very strange things may be going on here and I wondered if you might be able to help me," Melody asked.

"What things?" Russ asked, now fully awake, alert, and alarmed.

"I'd rather not talk about this over the phone. It may be ridiculous. Maybe my imagination is out of control, but on the other hand there might be something horrendous going on here."

"Do you want me to meet you in Phoenix?" Russ' words tripped out rapidly.

"That would be wonderful. I know it's a lot to ask."

"I'll call you from the plane."

Russ had to reschedule three meetings in Atlanta and give up his highly anticipated weekend of solitude, but none of that mattered. He just couldn't ignore a plea for help from a woman who made his heart leap, his hands sweat, and other body parts flood with excitement at the sound of her voice.

There she was, waiting in the terminal, lovely in jeans and a black top. Her arms were crossed just under her breasts. Tension seemed to radiate from every inch of her skin.

"Russ," she said. Her friendly hug setting the tone, sending a no-nonsense message.

Not quite as remote as a handshake though, Russ thought.

"Let's go," she said, her worry obvious.

"You're in charge here, ma'am," Russ said with a grin.

Melody managed a smile and Russ relaxed a bit. It was just plain comfortable being with Melody. Comfortable as a cowboy with a hard on, sitting next to the woman who'd caused it, commanding himself not to touch her.

"How was your flight?" Melody asked.

"The ride was fine, the pretzels left a bit to be desired."

"How about something to eat?"

"Some real food would be good. A burger 'n' a scotch."

Just being with her in her car, on her turf, was more stimulating than he'd imagined.

"Here's just the place," Melody said as she pulled her new white Jeep Cherokee into a parking space in front of a rustic cabin-like restaurant.

The place was dark and woody. Wood plank floor, wooden booths, wood panel walls with a moose head here and a fox head there. Candles in miniature galvanized buckets lit each table. Very masculine yet very intimate. The place was nearly empty with the exception of four loners gathered at the bar.

Russ followed Melody to a booth near the front corner window, as far from the men at the bar as she could get. A waitress sauntered over and Melody ordered a drink. Russ ordered the same plus a hamburger and fries.

"Thanks for coming, and on such short notice. I've discovered something strange. It's a long story and I don't know where to start."

"Start anywhere you're comfortable."

"This is all confidential, of course. You can't tell a soul." She laughed. "I'm talking to a reporter and the ground rules are complete confidentiality. Are you comfortable with that?"

"That's like asking a starving man not to think about food. All right. You have my word," he said, raising his his right hand in a three finger Boy Scout salute.

Melody took a breath. "I think there are some questionable things going on that have to do with the Scottsdale Anti-Aging Clinic and Marisa Fisher's husband's death," she whispered.

Russ was surprised. The clinic was now a leader in anti-aging treatment and especially anti-aging research. It was world renowned as the most prestigious clinic of its kind.

" Why? And why me? Why not the police?"

"I want to know more before going to any authorities. I think Stuart may be involved in some way. He's not been himself lately. I don't know why I think his state of mind has something to do with the clinic. It's just my instinct."

"I'll help if I can."

"It goes back to the trip Marisa and I took to Atlanta. Marisa found some capsules in her suitcase that were most likely her husband's pills. He died shortly before we took that trip and the suitcase had been his. I had the capsules analyzed by a friend who promised not to report anything until I have some more facts. It appears those capsules consisted of no known medical or experimental combination of drugs on the market. There were some medications commonly available in Europe that are not available in the U.S., combined with hormones you can get over the counter here and some that are by prescription only. But the dosage in each capsule was found to be way over the safe limit. There was also MDMA, or Ecstasy which is illegal and could cause a heart attack."

Russ took a long drink of his scotch, his interest soaring at what he was hearing.

"There's more. I've been spending some time down on McMannus Street—the homeless neighborhood here. On one of my earliest trips I saw people going in and out of a warehouse counting money. Not completely out of the ordinary, but I had a feeling something wasn't right and I didn't think anybody was selling drugs there. I've been back several times trying to find out what was going on. Finally, one day I got up my courage and went into the building."

Melody took a sip of her drink as she told him what had happened.

"Shortly after that, there was a hit and run car accident on 202 that killed the driver of a car just like mine."

"My god."

"And to top it off, a couple days later I was forced off the highway by someone ramming my car."

"You could have been killed."

"But I wasn't hurt."

"And you haven't told anybody about this?"

"Stuart and Marisa know about the accident and they know about the one involving the other car like mine, but I haven't told them about the last two trips to McMannus Street. The last time I was there, I was stunned when I saw a woman who had once been a patient of mine. Shows how great of a psychologist I was. Anyway, although she didn't recognize me, she told me what was going on in that upstairs room."

Russ leaned over the table as Melody continued to whisper.

"She said you go up there and they give you a shot and then you have to answer questions on a test. She said they also played a game. I think it's some kind of lab dexterity or memory test. I think they're administering drug tests and assessments up there with homeless people as guinea pigs."

Melody let out a long sigh. It all sounded much worse after hearing it out loud.

20

Russ checked into The Boulders and plugged in his laptop computer as soon as the door to his room closed behind him. He then began analyzing, organizing, and categorizing what he knew so far, leaving blanks that would need to be filled in as facts came to light.

When he had collected his thoughts, he fired off an e-mail to his boss that he had just received a lead on a very sensitive story that would be worth the time to investigate in depth. It could turn out to expose shocking abuse, he wrote, but it could also be nothing. If true, CNN would be the first to break the malicious misconduct and malpractice of a highly respected institution.

This investigation would have to be conducted objectively and surreptitiously, but in this case extra care would be required to keep his personal feelings out of the equasion. Melody had an effect on him he hadn't anticipated.

Later that night he began his first exploratory search, beginning with the unsavory task of going through the clinic's garbage. Disappointment reigned as he catalogued the detritus he rummaged through. Nothing seemed to be out of order from what he found.

Next morning, after a few hours sleep, Russ was watching delivery trucks come and go into the clinic's grounds while sitting by the windows at Wendy's across the street. Sometimes investigating is an unbearably slow, lonely job, giving the solitary observer too much time to think. Too much time for minds to wander. Russ' mind continuously wandered to Melody and whether he would ever see her again when this investigation was over.

Russ would maintain a businesslike distance from Melody as long as that was what she evidently wanted. He'd hoped for more, but he knew she was married and he wasn't one to fool around with married women.

Squeezing his eyes shut tight, he tried to wipe out images of Melody and went back to observing the clinic and playing with his breakfast. Playing with his food could only last so long. Russ soon finished, got into his car, turned on the air conditioning, and sat in the parking lot, his eyelids getting heavy. His vision nearly glazed over. Suddenly he spotted a Southwest Hazardous Waste Management truck pull into the clinic's driveway and disappear around the back. Russ quickly crossed six lanes of Scottsdale Road traffic to the clinic's driveway, following the truck.

The driver, in something resembling a space suit, got out of the truck and put four red plastic bags into a bin in the back. Russ copied down the name of the company.

With Russ in town beginning his probe into the facts Melody had put together, or more correctly, his investigation into the parts of Melody's theory that were nearly beyond belief, she neeeded to use all her bearing to maintain a state of normalcy and hide her anxiety.

Stuart looked intently at Melody with serious, sad eyes as they were having diner at Chompies. Breaking the silence between them, he asked, "What would you think about spending a few days at the Grand

Canyon together? It's supposed to cause some kind of revitalizing effect, or so I've heard from people who've been there. I think we need this right now."

Maybe this would be a good time to sort things out, Melody thought to herself. "When we get home we'll find a date that'll work for both of us. I love the Grand Canyon and you're right, there is something inspiring about it. I haven't been there since college. It's a good idea Stuart."

There was just a hint of a breeze as they left the deli and got into their car. They were both silent all the way home, Stuart contemplating when he could see Eva next, Melody planning to meet with Russ to find out what he'd learned so far.

The next day Stuart made a reservation at El Tovar for three nights: Thursday, Friday, and Saturday. They'd leave in three days.

Melody was surprised that he'd made plans so soon, but she was pleased. She loved the Grand Canyon and El Tovar was one of her favorite places on earth. Maybe time alone together in one of America's most magnificently beautiful and awe-inspiring locations would be just the ticket to get them in sync again. Maybe she'd confide her discovery of Grant's drugs and her fears of what might be going on at the clinic.

Tomorrow, she'd meet with Russ and see if he'd found out anything. Then she'd tell him her plan to include Stuart and suggest a meeting with Marisa.

21

"Marisa, it's Melody."

"Hey, I haven't heard from you in a long time, but I'm with a customer right now. I'll call you back in a bit."

"Okay, but call me as soon as you can. It's urgent."

Melody then got in her car and drove down to Marshall Way not waiting for Marisa to call her back. She found an empty parking spot right in front of the Three Sister's Gallery.

As soon as Marisa finished her sale, Melody hurried over. "Can you take the rest of today off?"

"What's so urgent? I'm here alone." Marisa said.

"I didn't exactly tell you the truth about what Jess found in those capsules." Melody said quietly.

"I just knew it." She folded her arms tight in front of her, then unfolded them.

"Marisa, I still haven't gotten to the bottom of it. I'll go over everything with you as soon as you can get off work."

"What'd you find in the capsules?" Marisa blurted out.

"Marisa, I've had to enlist help—"

"This was supposed to be between just you, me, and Jess. No one else."

"Lots of things have happened, and I needed help to sort through things that didn't add up. Please don't be angry with me. This goes a lot deeper than you'd ever have thought. Meet me at Tommy's at five. Okay?"

Marisa frowned and nodded silently.

Melody called Russ after she left the gallery. "Hi. It's me. Anything new?"

"Not too much. I need to talk with Marisa and ask her some questions about her husband. Can you arrange that?"

"She's meeting us at Tommy's this afternoon at five. Can you be there then?"

"Perfect."

Melody and Russ arrived before Marisa and found a booth near the back of the dim, nearly empty restaurant.

When Marisa walked in Russ was the last person she expected to see.

"Marisa, Russ is here because I asked him to help us. He knows how to probe and get answers."

Marisa greeted Russ with a small smile and a nod of her head.

"So," Marisa said, "what is going on?"

"Can I take your orders now?" interrupted their waitress.

"Scotch and water."

"Gin and tonic."

"Vodka on the rocks."

"There were two anti-aging components in Grant's pills that are commonly available in Europe," Melody said, "but not approved in the U.S. There was also phenylbutylnitrone which is an experimental drug and has not been approved by the FDA. There was way over the safe level of two hormones, DHEA and HGH. There was also a dangerous level of MDMA. The MDMA alone could cause a heart attack."

"What's MDMA?" Marisa finally asked, her voice shaking at what Melody told her.

"Ecstasy. It's an illegal sexual stimulant. Street drug," Russ said, looking down at the table.

Marisa was stunned as she covered her mouth with a trembling hand.

Melody and Russ gave her time to let the news sink in. Then Russ continued, "Marisa, we need to find out how Grant got those drugs. Do you have any idea who he might have gotten them from?"

Marisa shook her head.

"He was working with the clinic then, wasn't he?" Melody said to remind her.

Marisa thought a minute. "Yes. He got the account after meeting Eva."

"Eva?" Russ asked.

"Eva Blackwell. She's the biochemist in charge of the lab."

"Wait a minute. Eva is the biochemist in charge of the lab at the clinic and she was Grant's contact person?" Russ asked.

"I think she's a partner."

"Eva Blackwell has published a research paper on megadoses of the hormone DHEA — one of the drugs found in the capsules. I remember the name. I recognize it from researching the drugs found in Grant's capsules. I didn't know she was associated with the clinic. There was no mention of the clinic in the journal article. I guess it was written before her involvement."

"My god," Melody whispered.

Marisa remained silent, nearly in shock.

"Who else did Grant work with there?" Russ asked.

"I can't remember." Marisa's wide eyes stared into space. Searching her memory she came up with another name. "There's Greg Parker. He's the marketing director. That's all I can remember. I'm sorry."

"Well, here's what I've come up with so far," Russ said. "Maybe something will make sense to you. The clinic is regularly receiving shipments of mice. Nothing unusual there. But there was one shipping box that I found in their trash that was from Amsterdam."

"Amsterdam? So?" Marisa asked in a controlled voice that was on the verge of buckling. She bit her lip.

"My guess is that's the clinic's source for nootropilan and meclophenoxate. If they put that in Grant's capsule, it would be illegal, but it wouldn't be enough to prove them guilty of his death."

Marisa winced at Russ' statement.

"The clinic's been doing quite well. Why would they get involved in illegal drugs? I'm sorry. I wish I had more."

"It's way more than we had," Marisa said with a weak smile. "Thanks, Russ. What can I do that could help?"

"Do you remember how Grant got the Anti-Aging account?" Russ asked, looking from Marisa to Melody.

The two women looked at each other blankly.

"I'm not sure, but didn't somebody know somebody who knew somebody that tipped Grant off on the clinic as a prospective client?" Marisa said, finally. "Usually those leads come from builders or building suppliers, or media reps, or who knows. I don't remember."

"Well, I've got plenty more to look into. Can we meet again before the end of the week?" Russ asked.

"I'll be gone Thursday through Sunday," Melody said. "Stuart and I are going to the Grand Canyon for a long weekend."

Marisa raised her eyebrows.

Russ played with his napkin and said nothing.

"I'll be back Sunday night. Let's plan on Monday lunch.

22

Melody and Stuart drove north through the slow construction traffic on Interstate 17 until they finally reached the outskirts of Phoenix. They were each enveloped in their own solitary, pensive cocoon of thoughts. It seemed there was no way to begin any conversation, neither wanting to jeopardize the purpose of the trip: an attempt to save their marriage. One last chance.

"I can't wait to see the Grand Canyon again. You're going to be absolutely amazed by it." Melody said to break the silence.

"Mmm," was Stuart's only reply.

"We could stop at Sedona first, explore a little and have something to eat there, then continue up Oak Creek Canyon? Want to?"

"Sure." Stuart was consumed with visualizing where this four days together would lead. He was beginning to feel the whole idea had been a mistake. Every muscle in his body wanted to turn around and head back to Scottsdale where he could escape into the hot welcoming body of Eva.

How, he wondered, was he going to get Eva out of his mind

and be a loving husband to Melody on this four day trip? It had been months since he and Melody had made love.

As they left the desert and it's scrubby vegetation, ascending the four thousand foot incline toward Sedona, the drive that had started out wearisome and tedious became more congenial. The mountains, the tall pines, the clear air as they reached Sedona all seemed to change the atmosphere inside the car, somehow cleansing it of negativity.

After lunch at Tlaquepaque, they hiked part way up Bell Mountain and sat down, embraced by the intangible rays of affirmative radiance beaming down on them. There was no room for Eva in this scenario and her intrusive specter disappeared from Stuart's subconsciousness. This quietude was tranquil, tinged with hope and a whisper of tenderness. Unconsciously Stuart and Melody had clasped hands and time evaporated. Neither had an inkling as to how long they sat there. The past vanished and the future seemed to hold as much promise as the day they were married.

"My kingdom for this to last forever." Stuart whispered.

At that moment a group of tourists intruded on their idyll and returned them from ephemeral paradise to a hard rock in the hot sun. But the incident had already been captured and internalized.

It was time to move on. Oak Creek Canyon was verdant with mountain vegetation creating a canopy through which the curving, narrow road wound peacefully.

El Tovar in Grand Canyon Village hadn't changed a bit in the sixteen years since Melody had worked there between spring and fall semesters in college. In fact, it hadn't changed much since it's inception in 1904, except for upgraded plumbing and computerization. The expansive porch with arched stone openings wrapped around the entrance and three sides still invited guests to sit and observe the world through an opening to the past.

The dark Oregon pine logs in the lobby and restaurant echoed with the grandeur of an earlier elegance. A pre-income tax era where great wealth was accrued and permitted great extravagances while convention still dictated formality, protocol, and ceremony. When El Tovar was built, the raw American Western territories had only recently been opened by the completion of the Santa Fe Railroad. Although the concept of 'leisure' had yet to be discovered by most working class people, adventure was its precursor, and a trip to the Grand Canyon certainly fit the bill for adventure.

Melody was overcome by a sense of timelessness the instant she saw the familiar hotel. After finding a parking place she grabbed Stuart's hand and rushed up the steps into the lobby, impatient to share the enchantment she remembered so vividly. Melody loved the old lodge, all dark wood, soft lighting, and cozy ambiance, even with the dead animal heads on the walls eternally watching people come and go. She watched Stuart as he absorbed the atmosphere, hoping it would mean as much to him as it did to her. She watched as his eyes took in the huge moose head over the door of the gift shop, the massive carved wooden furniture, the carpets, and the dark beams. Yes, she thought, he'd been captured, too.

After soaking in the atmosphere of the interior of El Tovar, Melody thought about the canyon. She rushed Stuart out the front door to the south rim of the Grand Canyon for his first sight of nature's phenomenal creation. They'd missed the sunset and the canyon was dark, but the full moon created enough light to give them a faint hint of its incredulous size.

"Oh my god," was all Stuart could say, speechless at the majesty before him.

Melody sighed and put her arm around him. It was like old times. Everything will be fine now, she thought.

"I'll have the duck," Melody told 'My name's George, and I'll be your waiter tonight.'

"Prime rib, medium rare," Stuart ordered.

They toasted the promise of the days ahead.

"Think you're up to heading down Bright Angel Trail tomorrow? It's a beautiful hike. What d'you think?"

Stuart frowned. Although he'd only recently been consumed by thrill seeking, that phase of his life seemed to vanish after discovering the thrill of Eva. His idea of a get away to the Grand Canyon hadn't included anything physical. He'd intended it to be more meditative, reflective. Rejuvenating.

"Yeah, I think I'm game to hike down, but let's spend tomorrow exploring around the rim and then hike down Saturday. Another adventure to drink in before I die."

Melody was surprised by Stuart's remark, although his obsession with dying, or living, was nothing new to her.

"I think the Anti-Aging Clinic's making a real difference in my well being, don't you think? I could live to be a hundred, easy, if I don't fall off a cliff."

Not wanting to have any conversation about the clinic, Melody ignored the question. "Okay. Tomorrow we explore. Saturday we take the plunge."

Over dessert Melody silently wondered whether the night would be as promising as their first day had been. Maybe after all this time, all these celibate months, with stress left behind in Scottsdale, there would be a sexual rejoining of husband and wife. Melody was excited by the thought. She tried reading Stuart's face but he revealed nothing.

"What?" she asked, penetrating the silence at their small table.

"Hmmm? Nothing. Shall we go?"

Melody was nearly as nervous as the proverbial Victorian bride as they walked the quiet hall to their room. Stuart seemed to have retreated into that distant place that excluded her. Melody didn't know why it happened or what triggered his departure, but she felt him going away. No, not now, she willed silently.

"I love you, Stuart," she whispered, not meaning to say it out loud.

"I love you too," he replied.

When they were inside their room Melody decided the new moose robes she'd bought could wait for another time. As she rifled through her suitcase for her new night gown, she noticed Stuart take out his substantial cache of vitamins and herbal supplements packed in a Ziploc bag. They were only going to be gone for three more days, and it looked like he had enough for months.

She took a furtive look while Stuart was in the bathroom. Among the yellow tinged clear vitamin E's, orange vitamin C's, and dark, grainy health store looking caplets there were three white capsules. They looked the same as the capsules Marisa had found in Grant's suitcase. At that moment Stuart came out of the bathroom, catching Melody off guard.

"Did I scare you?" Stuart asked, a slight grin on his face.

"Yes, actually." But what's really frightening is what I saw in your bag of pills, she thought to herself. She smiled invitingly at Stuart, working hard to cover her fear.

"I want to make love with you," she blurted out fearing the worst.

23

"Oh, Melody," Stuart exhaled in a whisper as he tenderly approached her. He neither touched her nor answered her, but appeared to be searching for an escape. Stuart looked into Melody's eyes and kissed her softly on the lips. More than a friendly kiss, but less than sensuous.

He let out a low moan while he tried to push Eva from his thoughts.

Melody mistook this for passion. Encouraged, her pent up sexual desire mounted. She wanted him desperately, urgently, ravenously. It had been so long. Their intuitive understanding of each other's needs and desires seemed to have run off to some foreign, irretrievable place.

"Melody," he whispered, brushing soft kisses against her cheeks, her ear, her eye lids. He wanted to please her, to bring her to the heights of passion. But he was afraid to trust his own ability to make love to anyone besides Eva. He squeezed his eyes shut tight, pushing her vision from his consciousness. "Melody," he repeated more to himself than to her.

She wove her hands up his neck, through his thick, brown hair. The familiarity of touching him increased her desire for more. She held him tight, kissed him passionately, but his response was still tentative. She desperately wanted to feel the entire length of his familiar naked body against hers once again. Lovingly, she pulled away enough to pull her sweater over her head.

Still, he neither encouraged, nor protested. Melody's heart was pounding against Stuart's shirt when she again embraced him and pressed her lips to his, her tongue exploring the familiar taste. For an instant she thought she should stop to avoid rejection before it was too late. But she began to unbutton Stuart's shirt instead, still apprehensive. She looked into his gray green eyes for a clue, a direction, but he gave her no answers.

At that moment he reached up and unfastened her bra. Unsnapped her jeans. Unzipped her pants.

His touch set off fires long gone cold but not extinguished. Her breath caught repeatedly as some fragment of her insecurity escaped.

Slowly Stuart's body began to respond to Melody's touch, although he was barely aroused. As they lovingly continued their intimate foreplay, they rekindled long dormant desire and passion, once thrilling, then nearly routine, then nearly history, now fragile and cherished.

The quiet that followed their resurgence of intimacy was filled with physical satisfaction and ardent affection. Even love. Neither of them moved more than the rhythmic, repetitiousness of their synchronized breathing.

Melody was cooling in the afterglow of reuniting with her husband, her head resting on his shoulder, cuddled in the curve of his neck, pleasurably at ease after months of worrying about their future. This trip had been perfect so far. It had been reinvigorating just as Stuart said it might be. Yes, the Grand Canyon was undoubtedly Melody's favorite place in the world — especially right now. And they had three more days—two more nights before they had to leave and return to reality.

But had Melody been able to see Stuart's eyes, she would know that he was searching the darkness above him for answers to where the hell his life was going. He had a mistress he loved and a wife he still loved more deeply than he'd imagined. He felt like a juggler, required to keep unequal animate objects in motion, each demanding the most careful handling—the most precious position. If one fell, they'd all crash and he would have nothing left.

"Breakfast in the room?" Melody asked, invitingly wrapped in her thick moose robe.

"How 'bout breakfast in the dining room overlooking the canyon?" His suggestions always came out more like statements than questions.

The dining room provided a breathtaking visual treat. Stuart and Melody were seated by the tall windows overlooking the canyon. Stuart's first impression was of overwhelming majesty. The vastness of it surprised him. Of course he'd seen pictures of the Grand Canyon. Video, stills, paintings. But nothing prepared him for the enormity of it. Eons exposed by nature.

The sun was bright and the air clear. No haze to filter the vivid vermilion, cinnabar, and crimson. Vertical towers and pyramids loomed over the tiny river bed thousands of feet below, flowing through the yellow ocher, vanilla, and pale gold sandstone. Shadowy purples, dusky lavender, and periwinkle blue painted the shadows in the crevasses. The canyon walls were peppered with green scrubby piñon pines tenaciously clinging to life on steep, rocky slopes, some popping out of sheer cliff faces. And leafless, lifeless black skeleton tree trunks and branches remained as sentinels of the past. Long fingered plateaus. Mesas. Fissures. Chasms. All were spectacular.

"You're thinking we could hike down there?" Stuart asked. He stopped looking at the canyon long enough to leaf through the brochures they'd found in their room.

"People do." Melody's reply came off contentious, when she intended to be toying. "Would you rather go rafting? It'd be fun." That was better. Inviting.

"Let's take a walk along the rim trail and explore first. You've gone down before, right?"

"Yeah. A few times."

"How old were you?"

"Twenty."

"As in twenty with toned muscles and a good back? Twenty, as in prime cardiovascular functioning? Twenty with no sense of mortality?"

"Twenty as in daring, uninhibited, and easily talked into doing dangerous things just for the hell of it. It's not as bad as it looks. I promise."

"How about a helicopter ride? Ever do that?"

"Nope. Never have." Melody cocked her head as if daring him to ask her.

"Want to?"

"Yeah," she answered enthusiastically. "Yeah. Lets do that."

After breakfast they walked along the east rim trail, even spotting a California condor. They chatted with the few tourists they ran into. Some of them enthusiastically encouraged Stuart to make the climb down, telling him it was exhilarating, thrilling, and that he could buy himself a cap proclaiming to the world he'd hiked to the bottom of the Grand Canyon and back.

"I'll just buy the damn hat and skip the hike," he said laughing.

Melody took her camera and had a field day photographing people photographing the canyon. She took portrait shots of Stuart as she teasingly taunted him like most tourists taking pictures to take a step back, "one more, one little one more." Of course he didn't go anywhere near the edge. There were posted warnings everywhere. They'd read about five visitors who had fallen to their deaths in one year alone. But, still they joked and played and laughed and their love grew stronger than it had been since before....

Before what? Before Grant died.

The helicopter ride was breathtaking as the pilot did dips and sharp turns that made it seem as if they would crash into one solid rock wall and then another, then another. Not the typical tourist ride, but their particular pilot threw the thrill in at no extra charge. None of his passengers ever forgot their experience through the canyon in his helicopter. Melody snapped photos at angles she was sure had never been shot before—head on into a wall, nearly sideways around a pillar of stone. Jake, the pilot, had only been reported a few times, and usually got away with a requisite verbal reprimand.

Back on the ground they sat until the world stopped spinning, then they explored the village, watched the deer you're not supposed to feed, bought the damn hat and a few refrigerator magnets, books, and tapes, and laughed together.

It was a glorious day.

Melody had completely forgotten about the three suspicious capsules she'd seen in Stuart's things the night before.

24

Back in their hotel room, Stuart sat on the edge of their bed and watched Melody closely, wondering if they would have a replay of the night before. Making love to Melody had been a huge relief — a hurdle he hadn't wanted to approach but had cleared without a hitch. It was reaffirmation of his manhood.

Yes, he thought, he'd be able to continue his dual life. He also genuinely believed no one would be the worse for it.

It is fascinating what routes the human mind can conjure up to hold on to one's own self deception. What was once considered devious becomes only fair. Absurd grows rational. Borderline turns into acceptable. Never becomes occasionally. And tantalizing new paths open up, leading to even more involved, intricate self delusions. The old is let go, and the permeating losses suffered in this shuffle percolate so slowly as to be imperceptible until the past can't be contained any longer, and resurfaces unexpectedly, unforgivingly, unrelentingly.

"Stuart, those pills, your vitamins and stuff. Are those all from the Anti-Aging Clinic?"

"Why d'you ask?"

"I just noticed them last night, and I wondered what they're for."

"They're just vitamins and stuff. Why?"

Melody let out a sigh. "Come here. Sit down." Damn it, she thought. "There are some things I'm worried about. It's a long story."

"Well, tell me."

"Remember when we both thought there was something fishy about Grant's heart attack?"

"Melody, please."

"Stuart, listen to me. I think there's evidence that Grant was murdered," she said louder than she'd intended.

"Go on."

"Back when Marisa and I went to Atlanta," Melody said, "Marisa found some capsules in her suitcase that had obviously been left there by Grant."

"Why obviously?"

"Marisa said nobody else used that suitcase. She asked me to have the capsules analyzed and made me promise to keep it confidential."

"What'd you find?" he asked, edging closer to her.

"Stuart, the capsules looked just like the three white ones in your bag."

They were both silent for a long time.

"Now, what's in your pills and where did you get them?"

"What'd you find in Grant's pills?" Stuart asked, avoiding her question.

"There was meclophenoxate, nootropilan, DHEA, HGH, pregnenolone, phenylbutylnitrone, and MDMA," she breathed from memory.

"In English, please," Stuart said.

"European anti-aging compounds, hormones, and Ecstasy," she stated with the composure of an expert witness in a courtroom.

"And that could kill somebody?"

She didn't bite the bait he dangled for her.

"The quantities of hormones were way over the safe level suggested by the government."

"Oh, the government. There's a trustworthy source."

"And some of the drugs found in there are not approved in the states, plus, there was enough Ecstasy to cause a lethal heart attack in a healthy horse. Now, again, I'm asking you where you got those pills?"

Stewart felt like he'd been caught in a net. His storm gray eyes flashed with anger.

"All right. All right," he said with quiet resignation. He poured himself a glass of scotch from a bottle he'd brought with him. "I think you'd better join me."

Melody's heart was thumping. Stuart handed her a water glass three quarters filled with scotch and sat down in the chair at right angles to the queen size bed.

"This has been the worst year of my life. If the gods had told me what was in store for me, I think I would have bargained with the devil not to have to go through all this. Grant died. I've nearly lost the agency. You and I've had a lousy year. Lots of fights. No sex. And every day we're getting older. So I turned to the clinic for some anti-aging stuff. You remember I went there as a patient."

Melody nodded, agreeing with Stuart's assessment of the whole ugly year.

"They prescribed a bunch of anti-oxident vitamins and mineral supplements for enhanced brain and heart functioning and all that, and an exercise schedule which I never followed. But I swear nobody gave me anything that would put my life in danger. I assure you they're not that stupid. Eva's worked incredibly hard in her lab making important new discoveries — stuff that's about to change the whole face of geriatric medicine and human longevity."

"So Eva is behind this?"

"Leave Eva out of this," Stuart said too quickly.

Something in his voice changed Melody's concerns from anti-aging pills to something far from any previous thoughts she'd had. But it made sense.

"Are you having an affair with her?" Melody charged, the air she tried to breathe stuck in her throat.

"That's a stupid question," Stuart answered.

"Oh my god. That's why you've been so detached. That explains so many things."

"Melody."

Melody glowered at Stuart. "You were screwing your brains out with Eva. You nearly ruined your own business over her."

"I love you, Melody."

"You love me? You have a very strange way of showing it."

Both were frightened by what they'd said to each other. The hotel room that had been so grand the day before was now tomb-like, holding them hostage in a hostile square. The single queen size bed taunted the dismantled pair. The framed photos on the walls, showing eons of timeless beauty revealed by the Grand Canyon, mocked the rift in the world of Melody and Stuart that had occurred in a single rotation of the earth.

"Where did Grant get those capsules?" Melody added, regaining her composure.

"How would I know, Melody?"

"Who gave them to you?"

"Mine came from Eva. They're nothing more than some Chinese herbal stuff to help me sleep."

"Have you taken any yet?"

"No. And she'd never do anything illegal."

"You're a fool."

"What the hell are you saying? You think Eva is behind Grant's heart attack? That's absurd. She didn't even know him."

"Grant was involved with the clinic before you ever met any of them."

"There's nothing illegal or illicit going on at the clinic," Stuart said firmly.

"How'd you like to risk your life on that assumption?"

"You're losing your mind."

"Somebody who worked in the lab killed him with those anti-aging drugs. Wake up. There has to be a connection."

"Impossible."

Melody picked up Stewart's bag of pills. "I'm going to get these analyzed, and if I find the same mixture, you'll know you've been had. I might just be saving your sorry life."

"No!" Stewart sprinted in front of her, grabbed the pills, and rushing into the bathroom, he flushed the pills down the toilet. He then turned to face her. "I won't let you jeopardize all the good Eva's doing because your lame brained imagination has gone wild."

"It doesn't matter. I'll get to the bottom of this without your pills," she retorted. "I believe the clinic is involved in illegal, unauthorized human drug testing."

"That's absurd."

"And I'm determined to get whoever it is that planned such despicable behavior behind bars. You may even have been next on their list. I'm calling the police in the morning."

"No, you can't do that!" A menacing silence filled the space between them. Then Stuart broke into a hollow laugh. "Good luck finding something that doesn't exist."

Melody grabbed her jacket. "I need some air." She slammed the door behind her as she headed toward the rim path.

25

The moon was low and round and through the crystal clear night air the face in the once mysterious moon was unmistakable. The man in the moon who was once the source of fable and fantasy was now explored and scientifically mapped. Nothing stays the same — whether it seems the same for millions of years or a minute.

Melody was reeling from finding out that Stuart had been unfaithful. Had lied to her. She'd trusted him. He'd broken that trust, and that break could never be undone.

She felt the ultimate fool. She remembered seeing Stuart and Eva at lunch at Sammy's and now understood Stuart's flustered behavior. How could I have been so blind? So stupid? she thought, tortured from her heart to her fingertips. "He lied to me!" she confided to the empty canyon in a whisper. Her emotional strength was zapped.

Everything she'd once believed seemed to be questionable now. If she'd been so wrong about Stuart, could she be wrong about Grant? Maybe his heart attack had been truly an unfortunate, untimely heart attack. No way. Someone had drugged him. Was it Eva? Had she and the clinic involved any other unsuspecting people? What about those homeless people Molly McGinnis told her about?

"How could he!" Melody agonized, as visions of Stuart and Eva thrashing together in bed played through her mind. She and Stuart had been so in love. They'd laughed and loved and shared hopes and dreams. Or had they really? Lately they hadn't shared their thoughts at all. He'd been living in a double life and she'd had no clue. Then again, she too had withheld things from Stuart—her photographs, her investigation with Russ. An audible sob escaped from her heart. They hadn't shared their dreams. Had there been a beginning to this ending that she should have perceived long ago?

Stuart hadn't wanted to 'share' her with children, but he had no qualms about her sharing him with another woman! What an ass! What a bastard! What a lying, cheating, fucking son of a bitch.

Would I be better off without him? Will I be better off without him? Melody felt wobbly and weak and sat on a bench in the moon light. She couldn't imagine life without Stuart. She couldn't imagine life any way but the way it was. The way it had been until minutes ago.

Tears suddenly filled Melody's eyes and silently overflowed down her cheeks. She prayed for her mind to go blank and stop flashing images of Stuart and Eva together. Nude. In her bed?

At that moment her mother's voice popped into her head, with her often repeated platitude: Everything works out for the best, Melody, honey. "I don't think so, Mom. Not this time," Melody said outloud.

She then got up and walked mindlessly along the rim trail, looking at the shadows cast by the brightness of the moon. The solitude was comforting. The fresh air cleansing to her soul.

"Let go," she uttered. "Let go of the past. Let go of my old expectations of my future. It never would have been what I'd imagined anyway."

Stuart paced anxiously back and forth in their room, wondering what he might lose next. His sanity? He loved Melody, as crazy as he knew that would sound to anybody else with the exception of hundreds or thousands of misguided males juggling the same impossible combination of lover and wife.

What would Melody do now? Would she throw him out? Where would he go? Eva's? Did he really want that?

"Melody. I want Melody." A vision of Eva appeared then faded before his eyes, creating an excruciating sadness.

And then he weighed Melody's accusations. There was no way on earth Eva could ever have been the supplier of drugs that killed Grant.

But absurd as it was, the slight possibility was there. Stuart was angry at himself for not having hidden at least one of his capsules so he could have found out for sure what was in them, but he'd never in his wildest dreams foreseen what was going to happen. Better to have gotten rid of them all, he thought. Still, the question of what was in his capsules plagued him. Was there anything in them that might have killed him? Could Eva have intended to kill him? Was someone else using the clinic to knock off Grant, then him? "That's bizarre." Was someone messing with Eva's research, framing her? "Ridiculous!" But possible. Who?

Stuart sat on the edge of the bed, rocking back and forth unconsciously trying to soothe his tormented psyche.

He grabbed a room key card off the dresser and quietly slipped out into the night.

Darkness hugged the corners and niches the moonlight failed to touch. Stuart hadn't a clue where to go, but let his instinctive, intimate knowledge of Melody lead him. He walked up to the rim trail and then had to make a another choice—left or right? He listened to the quiet stillness surrounding him. He was frozen in indecision, then turned left.

Certainly if he didn't find her, she would eventually come back to their room. His lug soled shoes made no noise along the path. I love her, he thought. Nothing like the threat of losing something to clarify it. He continued walking slowly, seeing nothing, hearing nothing. Just as he was about to give up and turn around, he heard a rock bouncing from ledge to ledge. He followed the sound, and there she was, moonlight on her face, outlining her familiar, lovely profile. Her arms were folded in front of her, hands tucked under her arms.

He longingly whispered her name. "Melody."

She turned, not totally surprised that he had followed her outside. Stuart could make out her tear streaked cheeks, her puffy eyes, and waves of guilt mingled with desperation nearly smothered him.

"Melody." He sighed, words coming to his lips with difficulty. Fear of losing her gripped him. "I'm sorry. I'm so sorry for everything I've messed up. Everything I've done that hurt you knowingly or unknowingly. It's just been such an awful year for me. I've been crazy with grief and self pity. I'm sorry Melody. I love you. I do."

"The whole world changed tonight. Tomorrow I'll call the police and we'll tell them what I think is going on at the clinic. Then you and I..."

"No, Melody. You can't do that. We can talk about us, we can deal with what we have to deal with, but the clinic has nothing to do with our problems."

"You're right," she said angrily. "The clinic doesn't have anything to do with us. It has to do with the death of Grant, human experiments, maybe attempted murder of your own sorry ass."

"No, Melody, you can't! Promise me you won't call the police."

"Why? What are you hiding?"

"I'm not hiding anything. Just don't involve the police in the clinic. It won't do anybody any good and you'll cause unbelievable harm."

"I'm calling in the morning. It's the only sane thing to do."

Stuart snapped. Seemingly of their own volition, his arms reached up and without a thought or shred of control, he pushed her. Shoved her off balance and backwards into the darkness of the canyon.

26

Stuart was so panicked by what had just happened — what he'd done — that he couldn't make his limbs follow the commands of his brain. He wanted to see if he could rescue Melody, but he was paralyzed with fear and horror. The horror of what he'd done — he'd caused — engulfed him. This couldn't have happened, he screamed inside.

"NO!" he wailed to the heavens in a long, low, painful sob. Finally, he numbly rushed back to the hotel.

He sprinted up the five steps and crossed the porch into the lobby in a dazed stupor. The sleepy night clerk instantly sensed the signs of someone in shock. He rushed over to Stuart and put his wide, strong hand on Stuart's back.

"Are you all right?" he asked softly. He was afraid he already knew the answer. Tragedy in the canyon had happened before.

"Melody..." Stuart choked among sobs. "Melody...."

Without needing another word of explanation, the clerk quickly called 911 and set in motion the search and rescue operations that were routine to the rescuers.

By daylight, about four hours later, the search and rescue operation was underway.

"We'll do everything possible to find her," said Steve Smith, the ranger.

"You think she's alive?" Stuart asked, panic wraking his brain.

"It's always possible she could survive. There's always that possibility," encouraged Smith.

"Don't give up hope, Mr. Fox," Frank Bermont, the National Park Senior Criminal Investigator, said.

"Melody left the room to go out for a walk," Stuart began to explain. We'd had a huge argument. Said she needed some air. I waited — I don't know how long — then I headed out after her. I saw her on the trail," he uttered sadly, conjuring up the image.

The search began in earnest. Knowing where Melody was last seen and how long she'd been missing, search and rescue defined a geographical perimeter around where they determined the highest probable likelihood of her whereabouts would be if she had survived the fall. Then the area was partitioned into smaller areas marked by recognizable geological elements — that crevase, those trees, to the edge of that outcropping — for specific search groups. Ground searchers on foot, some with dogs, plus helicopters above, the rescuers began their difficult yet routine jobs. The terrain was steep and treacherous, but there was shrubby growth here and there that could soften a fall. Occasional piñon pines could block a body's decent. A ledge here or there that could stop a fall.

They would have had more luck finding Melody if Stuart hadn't lied about where she fell.

The search continued all day under the supervision of inky black ravens floating on thermal air currents, their piercing laugh mocking the futility of looking for Melody. The Steller jays, blue as brilliant sapphires with crested heads added their noisy call to the cacophony of the canyon's inhabitants. Peregrine falcons swooped and dived searching for swifts and swallows while the teams of rescuers combed the grounds for signs of a survivor.

At day's end the searchers convened at the ranger station to be debriefed.

Nothing.

They would continue tomorrow, broadening the search area to include more of the canyon.

Approximately fifteen hours had passed. Sun up was twelve hours away. She had to be found soon, or the search would revert to search and recovery rather than search and rescue.

Night time was agonizing for Stuart. Every time he closed his eyes, a repeat of his incomprehensible act replayed itself over and over in the dark of his room. Even with his eyes open visions of Melody falling thousands of feet like a broken doll tormented him. It was an accident, he repeatedly screamed silently to each excruciating replay his mind forced him to watch.

Stuart got up and went to the mirror over the dresser and took a long, deliberate look at himself. His imposing posture and demeanor had faded over the last half year with his ever increasing losses. He had worn his success flagrantly when he'd had it, and his confident looks had eroded along with his prestige. But he looked like the same man who had a loving wife just two days ago, although he now was a frazzled man who felt like his life was in complete chaos.

Could guilt be read in the shadows of his face by the criminal investigators he'd been talking to?

"It was an accident!" he authoritatively addressed his reflection. "She fell."

27

Marisa first heard about the tragedy on the Sunday night news. But before she'd had a chance to digest the unfathomable report, her phone rang.

"Marisa, it's Russ."

"Russ! Did you hear?"

"I can't believe it," he replied. "Can I come over?"

"Please," Marisa answered. She gave him directions and in the time it took him to get there, she tried to hold on to the hope that Melody was still alive.

Never grieve for the living, she remembered hearing many years ago. It was a perfect thought to get her through this night.

There was a light tap on the door and she hugged Russ tearfully at the threshold.

"Has Stuart called you?" Russ asked when he got inside.

"No. I should call him." She replied as she dialed information and got the number for the hotel. "They said he's unavailable," Marisa said as she hung up. "I want to drive up there first thing in the morning."

"You should be there for Melody, Marisa. Can you do that?"

"Yeah. Do you think Melody told Stuart her theory about the clinic?"

"Probably. That's what worries me, plus I've learned a few more things in the last few days. For one, Stuart's having an affair with Eva Blackwell."

"Not surprising. Do you think he told Melody?"

"I'll bet he did. And, to top that, Marisa, I'm being followed," Russ continued. "I lost them, but it's disturbing to say the least. I called the chemical manufacturers in Amsterdam, the one I found on a shipping label, and ever since then I've been watched. UPS deliveries to the clinic have stopped completely. Haven't had a shipment of any kind since I made that call. Something's going on they don't want me to find out. Maybe Stuart knows and realizes that Melody's right on the money."

"Then you don't think Melody's fall was an accident?"

"I'm ninety-nine percent sure it wasn't. Maybe I'll go with you tomorrow."

"I don't think so. If Stuart's involved and he sees you fishing around he'll shut down tighter than a bank vault. Eva and Stuart probably have their next step planned anyway."

"I brought a list of the clinic's employees, past and present. Would you take a look and see if any name means anything to you?"

"Sure," Marisa replied as Russ pulled a list of typed names and addresses from his jacket pocket. Marisa skimmed the list.

"There's a Laurel Greer on this list. Ex-employee. The name sounds familiar. Greer doesn't mean anything to me. There aren't a lot of Laurel's around. I don't know why, but that name seems to be the only one that rings a bell. Sorry."

"I'll check into her anyway. And I think it's time I confront Eva with a few questions."

With that, they both lapsed into silence and sat quietly, just for the comfort of another living, breathing person waiting for news about a person dear to them both.

"Are you in love with her?" Marisa suddenly asked.

"I don't know," Russ answered slowly, caught off guard. "I've never felt like this about a married woman, I'll admit that." He was embarrassed but happy to finally air his feelings.

Marisa smiled at the man next to her. She had known that he cared for Melody from the minute she saw the two of them together in Atlanta.

"I wouldn't consider Melody a married woman any longer. Once she gets back, and she will, she'll be heading straight to a lawyer's office if I know her. It hasn't been a happy time for her."

Russ relaxed as Marisa continued.

"She wants a family more than anything, and Stuart doesn't want kids."

"I'd love to have kids. Came from a family of four boys."

Marisa smiled broadly. "Give me your cell number again so I can get in touch with you the minute I have good news. And don't you dare think anything but positive thoughts."

28

A chipmunk sat on his haunches, staring at the intruder. The intruder hadn't made a sound or moved in quite a while. The chipmunk was curious but careful, and stayed a safe distance from the unmoving human. No chattering. No movement except for the flickering of his tail every so often.

Then an eye fluttered and a groan emerged from the human, and the chipmunk disappeared.

Melody couldn't remember where she was or how she got there, then it all came back to her in a rush of recalled images she'd thought had been a nightmare. She could see the sky and the tree that had broken her fall and saved her life. She could see the edge of the stone ledge just beyond the tree. Painfully she turned her head and looked down a sheer rock face of about three hundred feet to more rocks below. Turning back, she stared up at a steep wall of rock and shrubby trees.

He pushed me! He pushed me into the Grand Canyon, she recalled with incredulity. She was flooded with anger, consumed by a rage pierced by shards of sorrow and pain.

Then, in spite of her rage, Melody rotated each shoulder, one at a time. They moved without too much discomfort. She splayed her fingers. Curled them. Wiggled them and breathed a sigh of relief. Finally she wiggled her toes. At least she wasn't paralyzed.

Slowly Melody brought herself up to a sitting positing and grabbed hold and kissed the life saving tree. She took a deep breath and began to sum up her condition.

Her leather jacket was torn in several places, but had probably saved her at least that many cuts on her upper body. There was a long, bloody gash on her upper arm. Now that she was aware of her injury, a damn sharp, painful stinging began. Her knuckles were all bloody, but as long as her fingers worked, her knuckles weren't a major concern.

She felt very lucky. Surviving an attempt at being murdered by one's husband was a piece of good fortune, although not having been pushed in the first place would have been her first choice.

Being picked up by search and rescue within the next five minutes, that would be real luck, she thought to herself.

Why had Stuart tried to kill her? Eva. Stuart had admitted having an affair. But he could have divorced me, she thought. He certainly didn't have to try to kill me. Murder me. Then she remembered Grant's white capsules. Stuart's capsules. The clinic. Human testing.

I was determined to blow the whole thing open. She recalled her words precisely. For that he tried to kill me?

At the distant whir of a helicopter, Melody immediately felt revitalized.

"I'm over here," she yelled and waved. But with her energy depleted, her yell came out more like a whisper, and even that made her head throb terribly. Despair began settling into Melody's will like water in sand as the helicopter moved on. She quickly, consciously made her despondency stop, realizing that despair alone could do her in now.

Melody then released her grip on the life saving tree and eased back from the edge of the cliff. Looking up, she wondered how she'd survived.

A sense of immortality, not an uncommon response among survivors of death defying acidents, gave rise to confidence that she was meant to survive.

She surveyed the terrain and realized she couldn't climb up the sheer cliff face nor climb down from the ledge she'd landed on. To her left there was a ledge about a foot wide and from there she could climb down a bit and reach the Bright Angel Trail which she could then hike back up to the park.

Her stomach growled and her mouth was parched. She conjured up mental pictures of bottled water and a big breakfast around the bend. The sun was up in the east, casting the little ledge in shadow, contrasting with the brightness of the depth below. She turned face to cliff, nose to rock, hugged the jagged slope and stood up, every muscle making its aching presence known. Her legs buckled under the weight of her upright body. Examining her lower extremities she saw bloody scrapes and bruises on her legs. Nothing was bleeding at the moment. Her left ankle was sore and swollen, but as she slowly tried putting more weight on that foot, she was relieved to find that it wasn't broken.

Suddenly, her previous sense of invincibility vanished. Carefully Melody slid her right foot sideways about three inches, and she could sense the brink of the path. Melody convinced herself that would lead to safety once she made it across.

Her left foot followed, painfully and only slightly wobbly, while her hands searched for something to hold onto. There was a slight crevasse that she slipped her fingers into that helped her maintain her balance.

Her right foot slid two more inches to the right. Her legs began to shake as she again sought a handhold along the face of the cliff. Left foot, two inches.

Forward. One foot then the other. Inch by inch. As she made her way around the bend to the imagined breakfast waiting for her, the ledge narrowed. She could only get her toe on the ledge. Her heel was over air. She searched for a good hand hold to help her keep her balance and she found a protrusion from the cliff. It was sharp and cut her hand, but she didn't let go.

I can't do it, a little girl voice from her past moaned to her, tears beginning to well in her eyes. Yes, I can, the adult Melody's inner voice responded sternly. You can do anything you set your mind to, she recalled her fourth grade teacher telling her. And that dried up the tears.

She slid her right foot two more inches. The skinny ledge widened out. Enough to step on firmly.

Her hands were sweating and her legs were shaking.

"Bacon and eggs, buttery frosted cinnamon rolls with raisins." She slid another two inches with her right foot. She could see it would take about four more two inch shuffles. "Coffee! Orange juice. Ice water. Left foot, march," she ordered her sore ankle to follow directions.

The next step took her partially into sunshine which reflected off the rock face next to her cheek, nearly blinding her for an instant until her pupils could adjust. The heat felt good on her face, but sweat ran down between her breasts and down her back, tingling and itching. She had to stop to balance enough to wipe the perspiration from her hand on her pant leg, and try to stabilize her shaking, overtaxed muscles.

The little ledge extended out another two inches. There was a small triangular rise in the ledge that had to be bridged. It was too steeply angled to stand on. She skirted her foot over the rocky rise and found the continuance of the shelf that was her lifeline, only she hadn't stepped far enough to leave room for her left foot on that side of the rise. Her right foot had to move farther which would set her off balance. It took a baby step of her left foot and a baby step of her right then another sequence of baby steps until there was room for her left foot to join her right past the triangular stone rise.

One more step. Easy. Steady. Her right foot slid to the right. Left foot followed. The cliff her face had been hugging receded while the lip she'd been traversing widened out and Melody had enough room to lie down and regroup.

She lay there until the shaking subsided. Her head was still throbbing and she was thirsty, especially now that she had moved onto a sunny outcropping.

Something about a hundred feet away caught her attention. She crawled over to it, still too weak to trust her legs.

It was a discarded half full bottle of water. She slowly drank the hot water, soothing her parched throat.

"Let him think I'm dead," she said outloud.

"Bastard!"

29

More than once Melody slid roughly on her backside after losing her balance on rocks that littered the way. Melody was not only out of shape, but sore, hungry, thirsty, weary, scared and above all, angry. Determination to survive was still the strongest of her mixed emotions.

Once she reached Bright Angel trail, she sat down on a rock. Climbing up was definitely the shorter route, she thought, but she also knew it would take at least three times the effort to go up than to go down. Suddenly she remembered there was an emergency phone at the bottom of the trail. Four hours from here if all goes well, she reminded herself, although probably a bit longer now than when I was fifteen years younger and used to go down.

With the peace that came from making her decision, she curled up in a ball with her head on her jacket, hidden by the low branches of a hundred year old juniper. Listening to the noisy helicopter in the distance, she fell asleep.

When she woke it was dusk. Melody gathered her spirits, her aches and pains, her water bottle, which by now was less than half full, what was left of her energy, and slowly set out for the bottom of the trail where she would call for help.

She had no sense of time or distance as she mechanically put one foot in front of the other. The moon was waning, but the stars were brilliant. "Star light, star bright, all the stars I see tonight, I wish I may I wish I might. Get me out of this place!" she screamed.

Her head throbbed, and her arm ached from the gash while at the same time her anger grew stronger, deeper, consuming her, compelling her to continue. "Son of a bitch."

Finally Melody reached the Three Mile Resthouse where there was potable water. To her horror, the water had been turned off, tourist season being over. It was a bad omen. Melody pictured the phone at the bottom and prayed that it wasn't turned off as well.

It had been the middle of the previous night that she'd been so underhandedly pushed to her supposed death, and it was the middle of the night again. "I'll be damned if I'll go through all this and die. I'll make it out of here alive if it kills me!" she swore. She was now only as far as Indian Gardens. About three more miles if she remembered correctly. On a normal flat sidewalk that would be less than an hour at a leisurely stroll.

She sat on a boulder to rest for a minute and felt a pair of eyes looking at her. Small piercing eyes studying this human. A ring tail. I'm bigger than he is, Melody reminded herself. As he shot from his perch Melody jumped, a scream caught in her throat. The ring tail's appearance reminded her of the creatures living in the canyon, and she was motivated to move on.

She listened to the hoot of an owl and the croak of a tree frog in the distance, aware that the canyon was home to big animals, too. Deer, big horn sheep, and an occasional mountain lion. There were also harmless lizards and not so friendly scorpions and rattle snakes.

She had to reach the river before daylight. It's all downhill, she reminded herself, and dug to the depths of her physical and spiritual resources to continue.

"Bastard!" she cursed into the moonlit night, as she got to her feet.

She reached the Devil's Corkscrew where she eased herself through cactus, Mormon tea, and narrow-leaf yucca. It was hard for her to focus on anything but pain and hunger and her desire to sleep as she numbly continued, stopping for a moment to drink the last of her water.

Fear boldly gripped her as she began to doubt her ability to hang on. Then she forced herself to imagine a heartfelt welcome, at least among her friends, as she returned from the presumed dead. She remembered stories of unbelievable strength in the face of impossible odds — walking through blizzards to save a spouse or child, holding on to a drowning victim in a flood, escaping the fury of fire and smoke to rescue someone. When she got out, she'd be among those strong heroes fables are made of. Maybe not in reality, but the vision worked to keep her going.

Pipe Creek. Thirsty as she was with water at her feet, she knew it was contaminated.

Despair filled her weary bones. Suddenly she remembered that Pipe Creek wasn't far from the river resthouse. She could make it.

She was numb as she finally got there and collapsed near the river. The moon had set and five thousand feet above her the first streaks of crimson, violet, and lavender daybreak were just becoming visible.

The ranger station and phone were still too far for her to get to. She collapsed on a semi-smooth alcove among the black rocks, and she was soon fast asleep.

"Hello?" Was she dreaming? "Hello," the male voice repeated.

Melody slowly opened her eyes and looked up at a tall, gaunt, bony young man staring down at her, blocking the sunlight from defining the stockier shadow of another man behind him.

"You okay, lady?"

"No," Melody whispered through dry, parched lips. "Please help me." She was pleading to what she feared was a figment of her imagination.

The lanky young man seemed disturbed at having found her. He shifted his weight from one foot to the other and all ten of his fingers twitched at his sides. He'd have been more at ease if he had found a wounded deer or come face to face with a mountain lion. He couldn't leave her there and didn't know what to do with her. The stockier man was obviously displeased at what appeared to be another major hitch in their progress. He removed his baseball cap and resettled it on his red mop of hair at least three times in a row, wiping his forehead with his arm between each repetition.

"I won't go away," the lanky man responded.

"Here's some water," the stocky man said. "Just a couple swallows at first."

Melody filled her mouth with the precious liquid, letting it slide down her throat, as savored as a drink of the world's most expensive wine. Then another long, luxurious gulp, and the bottle was taken from her.

"I'm Lance Godfrey. This is Simon George. Are you in any pain?" Lance asked.

"Just my ankle and my arm—my head and every other square inch of my body."

"Let's have a look at that arm," Simon said with a slight British accent as he bent down to investigate the inflamed cut. "I'll get the first aid kit in the raft."

Lance nervously waited for Simon to return and then he ripped away the remaining fragments of Melody's jacket sleeve. He winced at the sight of the gash as he very gently cleaned it and spread salve from the kit.

"You must've taken quite a bloody spill," Simon George said, hoping his question would be answered with a simple answer so the two rafters could get back to their business of research.

"We're going to call for emergency help, and you should be out of here in no time. You'll be fine."

"No! Don't call." Melody desperately wanted to get out without Stuart knowing she was alive. "Please take me with you."

"We're already low on water since Simon's raft flipped and went on down the river without him. We don't have much food left either, and it's at least another two days of rafting to get out of here. Rations will be sparse and you're already weak. Are you sure you want to go with us?" Lance questioned.

"It won't be an easy voyage, I can assure you," Simon said in his British clip.

"I want to go with you. Thank you. I'll pay you when I get home. I promise. Please."

30

Past a brilliant sunlit wall, the raft floated calmly around a bend into a dark canyon of purple shadows nestled by rock walls rising thousands of feet up. Quiet. Beautiful. Peaceful. Golden sunwashed rock occasionally festooned with lucious green maidenhair ferns. Waterfalls cascaded over abutments sculpted slippery smooth by centuries of wear. Dark grottos were overshadowed by cliffs of limestone and shale.

Not more than two minutes past that peaceful place, Melody heard the sound of rushing water ahead.

The two experienced rafters braced for the oncoming rapids. Then the small overloaded raft began to pitch and yaw. The bow canted up and over the crashing, roiling waves while the stern dipped below water level. Lance and Simon paddled furiously to keep the three of them safe among the rocks and currents. Melody held on for dear life.

Finally, they passed through, exiting into calm water where Melody resumed breathing. Just as she'd relaxed enough to regain her confidence, she heard the ominous distant roar of more rapids, the rumble of pounding energy. The river suddenly narrowed, held back by two flying buttresses of rock. Slipping past the monumental structures they now faced a wall of vigorously churning raging rapids once again.

The raft rose up with the turbulent water and crashed down sideways, toyed with by the capriciousness of the Colorado River. The noise was deafening. Melody breathed in a mouthful of water. Choking and sputtering, she maintained her balance. Again the bow was tossed high into the fury, followed by a fall that left the stern, as well as Melody's stomach floating on air. Again and again the boiling currents manipulated the raft high into the air then brought them crashing back down into the roaring, powerful river.

Then suddenly, just as Melody had begun to wonder if she could maintain her sanity, they came to a peaceful resting place and pulled the raft onto dry ground for the night. On a soft, sandy beach, Melody fell asleep on the balled up remnant of her jacket she still clung to like a memorial to her past, safe, life.

"Gee, she didn't even thank us," Simon said as he stood looking at the pile that was Melody's still body lying curled up on the sand.

"Shut up, Simon," Lance replied. "She's just exhausted." He then got the antiseptic lotion and antibiotic cream from the first aid kit and redressed Melody's gashed arm. She didn't budge, responding like a rag doll to Lance's maneuvering.

When she woke, she was disoriented, but then memory flooded into her consciousness. Stuart tried to kill me. Melody quickly got to her feet and stared at the Colorado River, peacefully gliding past her.

Lance and Simon were busy with gathering samples and making notations. Melody was anxious to get back on the watery road and leave the Grand Canyon behind her. But she was at the benevolent mercy of the two strangers who happened, by chance, by timing, and by the whim of the universe, to be in the right place at the right time to be her life savers. How does a person repay another for saving their life? Forever grateful is a pathetically minuscule repayment. Money? How much is my life worth? And to whom, Melody wondered in a rising tide of self pity. Not Stuart. Her parents, certainly. Marisa, yes. Three people in the whole damn world.

Russ. Fond images materialized as brilliant as a kaleidoscope aimed at the sun. Russ. Memories of his eyes offering more than friendship while asking nothing in return. Her heart warmed, tempering the chill that had seeped into her bones.

"Coffee?" Lance asked as he walked up with a steaming cup. "It's not much, but it should help warm you up. Get your joints moving. All that's on the menu this morning is a bit of granola bar. We're down to minimal rations. Sorry."

Melody smiled up at the gaunt man offering her some of what little he had left. His kindness brought tears to her eyes.

"Thank you." She pushed the tears back and replaced them with sincerity. "You've been wonderful, is all I can say. If I ever have a son, I'll name him Lance."

Melody was sure she'd remember the embarassment on Lance's face for the rest of her life.

Just then Simon broke the spell. "Let's get moving."

Near dusk, the bleary trio arrived at Diamond Creek — the end of their river journey. Lance and Simon's truck was where they had left if for the final leg of their journey.

Hunger and exhaustion fought for the upper hand, and hunger unanimously won out. They drove until they spotted a cafe on the horizon.

As they sat down in a booth they found, to their delight, that char broiled steaks they'd been hoping for were on the menu. Lance and Melody were nearly delirious.

Then Melody began laughing. "I don't have a dime!"

"There's always dish washing," Lance said jokingly.

"I already owe you my life. Can we add a dinner to that debt?"

"Do I have a choice?" Lance asked.

Melody smiled at the two men and went over to the pay phone. "I'd like to make a collect call to Russ Daniels at The Boulders in Scottsdale, please."

31

Russ pulled into the parking lot of Stella's Cafe and immediately spotted Melody's profile through the dirt caked window. His heart skipped and he realized he was hopelessly in love with this woman who had picked him out of a crowd once, even if it was to escape an irritating conversation she'd wanted to end. An accident or a coincidence?

She was sitting alone, and Russ slid in the seat alongside her. Every centimeter of her dirty, dazed face expressed pain, exhaustion, incredulity, relief, and gratitude.

"I'm alive," she said. "Two guys in a raft saved my life." Then she smiled. For a moment her happiness at seeing the friendly face of Russ dissipated her aches and pains. A tear of great relief slipped from her exhausted eyes and etched its way down her cheek.

"Come on, let's go. You can tell me about it when you're up to it."

"Stuart pushed me."

"Marisa and I figured as much. Shhh. Come on now." Russ was as gentle as if escorting an elusive cloud as he put his arm around her waist and guided Melody out of the cafe and into his car.

She immediately fell asleep and didn't awaken until they got to Russ' hotel in Scottsdale.

"A toothbrush! A bath! Hot water up to my neck. I may never get out once I get in the tub. You might be able to bribe me with Tiramisu, coffee, brandy, and a soft pillow on a soft bed with silky sheets."

"Anything at all will be my delight. I'm so grateful you're alive."

Melody quickly filled the tub and sank into pure pleasure with clean, hot water swaddling her aching body. The gash on her arm stung, but even that was not a bad price to pay for the luxurious soaking she was enjoying.

When she heard room service knock on the door, there was a tug of war between her desire to stay and soak and her hearty appetite for some of what she knew Russ had ordered. Food won out: Tiramisu, hot black coffee, and brandy.

It all seemed unreal — being pushed to her near death by Stuart; her good fortune at having survived, and now, being clean and comfortable, wrapped in a soft terry cloth robe in Russ' hotel room.

"They're still looking for you, you know," Russ said, as he took a sip of coffee. "They found fragments of your jacket in the Colorado River but no body. They're looking, for your body, farther down river." The reality of what could have been an accurate statement had Melody not been sitting in front of him nearly made him choke with sadness.

By now, Melody had regained enough strength to tell what had happened: her argument with Stuart; finding the three white pills that looked just like Grant's capsules that Stuart then flushed down the toilet; Stuart's insistence that Eva wouldn't do anything illegal; and Melody's accusations that the clinic was involved in illegal human testing.

"Marisa and I were sure you wouldn't have jumped."

"Why would I jump into the Grand Canyon?"

"Stuart said it was because he told you about his affair, and you were beside yourself."

"How stupid. I think it might have been Stuart who fiddled with Grant's pills."

"Why Stuart?"

"I found a note in my office. I'd forgotten all about it until my brains were scrambled by the rapids. The note said 'NEXT.' Maybe Stuart killed Grant on purpose and I was next on his list."

"But why would he want to kill you or Grant? And why would he warn you?"

"I don't know. It doesn't make sense."

Russ then filled Melody in on his being followed and his discovery of drug shipments from Amsterdam. He then asked her to go over his list of the clinic's current and ex-employees.

"Laurel Greer! She's Stuart's ex-wife," Melody said, her heart in her throat. "Stuart and I lived together for a couple years, then he dumped me for her. He married her after they'd known each other for only about three months. They were only married a short time. He divorced Laurel because he realized he still loved me."

"What'd Laurel do at the clinic?"

"She was a lab assistant," Russ said slowly, as his brain hit fast forward. "Eva was her boss."

Melody gasped at the connection. "Stuart told me that Laurel said she'd never forgive him for using her to get over me. Stuart and I ran into Laurel occasionally and each time she made me uncomfortable."

"Did she ever threaten either of you?"

"I don't remember," Melody answered.

"When was the last time you saw Laurel?"

"I saw her at the airport before I went to Atlanta. She was going to Mexico to go scuba diving."

"Did Laurel and Grant have any kind of a relationship?" Russ asked.

"They were all friends when Stuart was married to her—Grant

and Marisa and Stuart and Laurel. Oh my god, Marisa—she must be worried sick. My parents…."

"Call your parents. I called Marisa while you were taking a bath. She was up at the Grand Canyon to be there when you were found. She's on her way back now. I told her not to tell a soul you were safe She should be here any minute."

"Melody! I'm so glad you're alive," Marisa said giving Melody a hug.

Then the two friends sat down as Russ repeated Melody's story. His words were laced with anguish as he related what Melody had been through. When he mentioned the capsules Stuart had flushed down the toilet Marisa gasped. "You saved his life, and he tried to kill you in return?"

"Could Laurel have been the connection that got the agency the clinic account?" Melody asked, as her friend calmed down.

"Of course." Marisa was speechless for a heartbeat or two, then continued. "Now I remember. Grant told me he'd been uncomfortable in her presence because she had such obvious hate in her eyes while she spoke lovingly of Stuart. He told me it was spooky that someone had hate and love so intricately laced together."

"It doesn't make sense that Laurel would be involved in giving Grant an overdose of drugs when it was Stuart she hated and loved," Melody said. She didn't have anything against Grant."

Then Melody thought for a moment. "But, if you loved and hated someone and you wanted revenge, how could you most hurt that person and not be suspected of any wrong doing?"

Melody and Marisa knew the answer at once.

Melody then turned to Russ. "Stuart and Grant were not only partners, but had become best of friends. More like brothers than friends. Being partners will either bond you together like a marriage or drive you to hate one another. They both used to say that ad nauseum. So how could Stuart's ex-wife hurt Stuart without laying a hand on the man she still loved? By killing his partner, best friend, and brother. She must have laced Grant's capsules. And I was supposed to be NEXT."

"Then it was Laurel! She killed my husband."

32

Laurel Greer was shocked when the doorbell rang, interrupting the late news on TV. She looked out the window by the front door. Although she wasn't expecting anyone, these visitors were the last people on earth she thought would come knocking. Her gasp was loud enough to be heard by the threesome on the front stoop.

Speechlessly she opened the door. Melody, Marisa, and Russ walked in without waiting to be asked.

"Melody!" Laurel forced a smile. Her eyes remained wide and filled with shock. "My god, you survived!"

"Good to see you too, Laurel. I'd like you to meet some friends of mine who've been just dying to meet you. You know Marisa. We wanted to bring her two sons, Eric and Josh, but they're already in bed, probably dreaming about their Daddy and remembering what it was like to have him tuck them in bed at night."

Marisa glared at Laurel. Being face to face with her husband's murderer was the most heinous moment in her life.

"And this is another friend, Russ Daniels," Melody continued. "He's an investigative reporter with CNN. We were just talking about you and he said, 'why don't we just go pay Laurel a visit.' So here we are."

Melody sensed she could make Laurel crack any moment now.

"We were talking about Grant and some pills Marisa found in his suitcase after he died."

"I don't know why you're here, and I hate to be rude, but it is late. Maybe some other evening."

"We're here to find out exactly why you killed Grant."

"I didn't kill Grant! He died of a heart attack," she protested. Then looking directly at Russ and Marisa, she continued, "You ought to take her to have her head examined before she does something that will really embarrass you. She's way out of line."

"You once worked at the Scottsdale Anti-Aging Clinic." Melody said.

"Is there something criminal about that?"

"What an appropriate choice of words. One of the things we're looking into is illegal drug testing by the clinic. Know anything about that?"

"I worked there for only a short time. I don't know what you're after, but I didn't do anything wrong."

"Just long enough to make sure Fisher and Fox got the account? So you could kill Grant?"

"I really think you should leave now."

"Why did you kill Grant?"

"Why would I do that?"

"We already figured it out, but we'd love to hear it from you. We know it was you who mixed the drugs and filled those capsules."

A clock ticked in the background, marking time. Just then a neighbor's dog barked loudly, piercing the silence, making Laurel jump.

Suddenly, lightening crashed and flashed through Laurel's house. Thunder roared, rumbled, and reverberated creating an eerie electricity as the wind kicked up and wailed at the windows, rattling them in their frames. Rain and hail pelted the roof as if it were a repeat of the storm that appeared out of nowhere during Grant's funeral.

Laurel looked from one face to another, as though pleading with Marisa and Russ to agree that Melody was crazy.

"How could you?" Marisa said over the roar of the storm. "You hardly even knew him."

"I didn't kill him," Laurel repeated, control slipping away.

Russ picked up the attack. "Was it you alone who killed Grant or is the whole clinic involved?"

"You're crazy. He died of a heart attack if you remember. Why are you doing this to me?"

"The heart attack was a direct result of the drugs you gave him. You wanted to hurt Stuart."

At that, Laurel broke. "I got my revenge, and it was sweet. I could have easily killed Melody first, but that would have only hurt him for a little while. Stuart would have gotten over you in a minute," she said, turning to Melody. "Stuart lost everything when Grant died. It was perfect. Stuart lost his partner. His agency. His status. He shouldn't have dumped me for you. That was his first mistake. But I didn't kill Grant. He died from a heart attack."

Marisa could hardly contain herself at those words.

"Maybe I did mix those capsules, but I didn't make Grant take them. He did that on his own."

"You are guilty of cold blooded murder," Melody charged.

"You're just fishing, and you won't get anywhere here. Get out of my house. You're all crazy."

The knock at the door came as a surprise to Laurel, but not to the others.

Laurel slowly went to her front door.

"Phoenix police, ma'am. Are you Laurel Greer? We have a warrant for your arrest."

Epilogue

"It isn't justice for one man to cause a woman so much heartache and then have him be free. Stuart Fox is the one who is guilty — guilty of causing unendurable pain and suffering and that was the crime." That was what Laurel Greer blurted out to the press after her conviction of premeditated murder. She is now spending life in the Arizona Women's prison, doing dishes and plotting her revenge.

Eva Blackwell was censured by the Board of Mental Health Commissioners and was prohibited from doing research for six months, nor to ever do any type of experiments involving humans. Eva spent her six month hiatus in Amsterdam studying the latest anti-aging medicines.

Stuart, with the aid of a high priced, cunning attorney, was not found guilty of attempted murder. As Melody had feared, the jury found that Stuart did not intend to harm her. It was determined to be an accident in the heat of passion. Stuart's advertising career was finished. The Fisher and Fox Advertising Agency was taken over by a new, savvy young woman who renamed the agency The Idea Bank and in her first year of business garnered five local advertising awards and two national awards. Stuart accepted Eva's invitation to spend her six months of censure in Europe with her. He died of a heart attack after spending one week with her.

Russ divides his time between being with Melody and wherever in the world he is sent. He was once hospitalized in China and nearly died after two weeks of hallucinations caused by an extremely high fever of unknown origin. His uncovering high levels of arsenic in the public water system in a small town in Mexico caused the death rate there to decrease by twelve and a half percent. He continues to investigate and report on world health issues and his television ratings have skyrocketed since reporting the illegal activities of the Scottsdale Anti-Aging Clinic.

Marisa started her own company which buys investment art for Fortune 500 companies throughout the country. She has been very successful and happy with her life. Although she still misses Grant and knows no one will ever replace him, she has met a man with whom she hopes to spend the rest of her life—but not yet.

Melody has given up photography even after her one woman show at the Three Sisters Gallery in Scottsdale was highly touted. She sold three photos to art museums in the Southwest, and received a humanitarian award from the National Alliance for the Mentally Ill. Her relationship with Russ has thrived and blossomed and she has never been happier in her life.

www.ingramcontent.com/pod-product-compliance
Lightning Source LLC
Chambersburg PA
CBHW011654010726
47499CB00010B/3257